More
Tales from a
Gimbaled Wrist

ALSO BY MICHAEL L. MARTEL

Tales from a Gimbaled Wrist

The Kapellmeister Conspiracy

More Tales from a Gimbaled Wrist

Short Stories and Other Reflections Concerning a
Lifelong Love of the Sea

Michael L. Martel

Edited by Nim Marsh

This printing 2012

Points East Publishing

For

Mom and Dad

"The Old Man stirs with an iron fist/
And the first mate drinks with a gimbaled wrist/
And the whole damn crew's got a thirty degree list...
Tanqueray Martini-O!

—Jon Campbell, *"Tanqueray Martini-O"*,
from his album *"Keep on Fishin'"*

Contents

Arise then, and go.
The salt mist hath kissed thy cheek,
Turning thy face seaward.
The scent of the Deep, cold, green, and cloying,
Hath found thee, Brine-sweet,
Flowing in with the flooding tide.
It calls to thee; Bestir thy limbs, now,
Make ready the ship;
With cheerful, curious, child's heart, cast off all lines,
And be borne, by tides and winds all favorable,
Outward, onto the eternal sea.

The Waypoint

In the noisy, turbulent darkness, sleepless minutes passed like hours. The big schooner yacht rolled, pitched, and yawed in the endless cobble-seas, creaking and slamming and rattling in constant motion while I lay in my berth, trying to remain immobile, trying to catch the barest, fleeting, delicious moment of elusive sleep while waiting for morning. I had grabbed every pillow of any kind available and jammed them all around my body in a vain attempt to immobilize myself, to little success; it was like sandbagging against a rising flood. We circled, sailing in a holding pattern a few miles off of Bermuda, in steep, gale-driven seas, waiting for daylight so that we could navigate our way past the deadly reefs that encircle the island, and find our way through the channel into Town Cut and St. George's. We were all chilled, wet, and weary and had been so for quite nearly a week.

At long last, I heard the diesel engine rumble to life, somewhere up forward in the belly of the vessel; and to my surprise, I realized that I had dozed, just a little; and through the little antique prismic glass window above, in the sky-light, I could see the welcome glow of the gray dawn, and it cheered me; my pulse quickened and heart beat in anticipation like that of a child. At long last, we were headed in. Still, I lay there in a few moments of peaceful contemplation, looking upwards at the sky through the glass. It was a high dawn, broken clouds of a mottled mackerel-scale ceiling far above and still well before the sunrise, but I thought it beautiful, and so much like the many daybreaks I had seen at sea in years past. Despite whatever conditions one has at the surface, a high dawn at sea is a time of peace, contemplation, and joy, even though it is usually a harbinger of strong wind later. But for the moment, a new day, with all its possibilities, challenges, and fears, is about to break, and the sun will rise.

Out of the dusty recesses of my mind came, inexplicably, a fragment of an old rhyme, and in the half-light, and it brought a faint smile to me:

> *"The evening red and morning gray,*
> *Are sure signs of a fine day…"*

1

A few hours earlier, on my watch, I had been up in the cockpit, counting down the last hour to go before midnight, and the watch change. I was wide awake, and excited. The classic 85-foot Herreshoff schooner was slicing through the seas, on a close reach, roaring ahead in a rising gale, but I felt confident now, because we were headed for landfall, and all the anxieties of the past week were dissolving as my mind focused in anticipation on only one goal; reaching Bermuda.

Seated in the cockpit by the wheel, with my back to the wind on a starboard tack, I watched the half-moon rise over the eastern horizon, cheerfully illuminating the flying crests of the building seas with a soft, silken glow reminiscent of a dreamy, romantically wild 19th-century oil painting of a seascape at night. Beethoven's Moonlight Sonata came to mind. But this was no still-life; this was very much a world in motion.

Every so often, a sea would break against the bow, sending invisible, dark spray flying aft to the cockpit; it felt warmer than the icy seas that had doused us for days, and tasted clean and briny. The motion was suggestive of the art of riding a horse; the boat moved in long and gentle, steady, measurable leaps through the seas. Odd, I thought, how pleasurable this particular moment is, this stretch of a few hours sailing so gloriously along out here in the middle of a trackless ocean, despite the physical discomforts and perpetual weariness, in the middle of the night when the rest of the world are comfortable in their motionless beds ashore.

We had been nearly a week on lumpy, cold November seas, en route from Newport, Rhode Island to Tortola, BVI. We had battled 40 to nearly 50-knot gales for three days, constantly wet, queasy, sleep-deprived, and chilled throughout. Now the skipper had decided that we should stop in Bermuda to refuel and repair a fresh water maker that wasn't working right. All four of us were ready for a break. We were tired of cold, strong gales, and rough, lumpy seas, and dearly sought a full night of sleep in still waters.

Distances at sea can be deceiving, especially at night. For a few hours now, we had been able to see the very faint, unnatural glow of Bermuda against the cloud ceiling in the distance. It was colorless and barely discernible, yet still visible against the absolute murky darkness all around. So I thought we were closer, when in fact we were still many miles distant, even too many miles for VHF radio contact; and over the next few hours that glow would grow

2

brighter and larger, eventually punctuated by the flashes of light tower beacons against the undersides of the clouds. The lights themselves were still beyond the horizon; yet the comfort that even that faint glow, no matter how distant, imparts to the mind, is powerful. It gives newfound strength and energy, and fosters a change of mind-set and perspective. Everything is transformed by a new inner light, a paradigm shift; the mind is indeed its own place, as Milton observed. I had never been to Bermuda; this would be my first visit, arriving under sail, at that, to this lonely outpost of land in the middle of the ocean, formed of ancient volcanoes, exposed seamounts, land that simply does not belong out here in the heart of Neptune's realm.

My eagerness was tempered with the recently gained knowledge that another 40-knot gale was brewing, and would be fully upon us within a few hours, in fact by morning. This created some anxiety for me. I did not want to be in another stiff gale so soon. I had begun to be able to pick up scratchy, static-punctuated weather forecasts from Bermuda Radio. The prediction was for the gale to blow out of the southwest. It was already blowing out of that direction and at nearly 25 knots at that, and was growing stronger by the hour. I looked at the chart, and had suggested to the skipper that since we were approaching Bermuda from the northeast, we would get relief by being in the lee of the island, where we could remain offshore in the shelter of the land until dawn, and then motor into St. George's harbor. The approach to Bermuda is complicated by the fact that the island of Bermuda itself, which is not really a single island but a collection of many small islands, all in close proximity – is surrounded by a 10-mile perimeter of deadly coral reefs and shallows. There are actually only two safe and reliable routes into the sheltered harbors of Bermuda. They both begin on the northeast side of the island, since no other approach from any direction is safe or possible due to the deadly encirclement of reefs. One can go into St. George's through a man-made cut channel, or follow another channel around the island and inside the encircling reefs, to enter Hamilton Harbor from the southwest via Great Sound. We were going through Town Cut into the harbor of the old and quaint town of St. George's. That was our destination.

My plan was perfect in theory, except that since I had not been to Bermuda before, I really didn't know how high the land was, and how much effect it would have in creating a comfortable lee from

3

the gale. It turns out that the land is rather low, without mountain peaks or anything of the sort, and as a result, the wind literally howls over the little archipelago as though it's hardly there. Couple that with the fact that one must stay well offshore, in the darkness, to stay prudently outside of the deadly reefs, and one might as well be out on the open sea, for all the shelter that its lee is worth.

"Whose idea was it to hang out here in the shelter of the island?" Captain Tom growled audibly that morning, as we motored in at first light. "There is no lee of this island!" But of course we really had no choice anyway. One does not try to thread the needle into Bermuda at night, not ever. Crewman Jay and I had argued. He wanted to get in close to the north end of the island, within a mile of the light marking the outer edge of the reef, Kitchen Shoal. It was our watch and I was the Mate; Captain Tom was asleep below, off watch. Since I had never been to Bermuda before, I felt that caution would be the best course of action, rough seas notwithstanding. "I'm not taking us in that close" I told him. "We should stay three miles off, at least." Jay disagreed emphatically.

Later, at midnight, when Captain Tom came on deck, he responded angrily to Jay, whose question I had not heard, but could not miss the response: "No! Absolutely not! You don't go into a harbor you don't know at night!" Captain Tom remonstrated, his voice raised. That was the end of that discussion. But then the skipper went beyond the point I had suggested to the east end of the reach, where the boat was once again partially exposed to the southerly swell, and we bounced and rolled around for about three and a half interminable hours until first light, when the sound of the engine starting roused me.

As we had been drawing closer, hours earlier, I heard the weather broadcast from Bermuda Radio increasingly more clearly. It was a live broadcast, it seemed, even though it was the middle of the night, delivered by a pleasant, professional radio operator at Bermuda Radio, a fellow with a British, if not decidedly Scottish, accent. Hungry for human contact outside of our vessel, and thinking, mistakenly, that my transmission might be heard as clearly by that operator as I could hear his, I tried to radio the operator, because the weather forecast transmission had been spotty and broken up, but the words "40-knot gales" had been quite discernible. I queried him about the forecast, and asked him to repeat it.

He came back to me by saying that we were still too far away for him to make out our transmission, and that we should contact the station again in a few hours when we were closer to the island; but he had heard me ask for a repeat of the marine weather forecast, and although he did not say so over the air, I believe that he detected some anxiety in my voice, and as a result, he quite remarkably, and patiently, repeated the forecast, speaking slowly and distinctly, a kindness and professionalism that I had not anticipated, and which of course would have been an impossibility with the automated broadcasts heard on weather radio here in the U.S. It was contact, though, and it cheered me even more, although that cheer was tempered by the validation of my concern, that we would be in the heart of another gale in only a few hours, long before we would be in the safety of the harbor. Well, I thought, we will simply have to make do, and manage. It would be a long, long night.

It was still blowing half a gale on deck as we motored around the channel markers and into the narrow cut – Town Cut – a channel blasted through a limestone cliff – and into a strange calmness that we had not known for a week. It was sunrise, orange, groggy, damp, fatigued sunrise, my mind dulled by lack of sleep, sights and sounds coming to me as through a frosted lens, fuzzy and dark around the edges. Scrubby trees like windswept evergreens hung on tenaciously to the rocky ledges around the harbor entrance and for the first time I realized that the strange sweet scent reaching my nostrils was the smell of land. Land does have an aroma, indeed, but one is not conscious of it until one has been away from it for a few days.

We passed through the cut and into the snug harbor lined with steep, close hillsides and pastel houses with tall palm trees between them. The strong wind sent low clouds scudding across the sky seemingly barely above the rooftops and the branches and fronds of every palm tree had been turned into a windsock. When I stood on the dock at the 18th-century stucco-walled Customs House, the solidity felt strange. I remembered one such morning on another island, St. Martin, and walking at sunrise to the little Patisserie on the inner harbor at Marigot, and a cup of strong coffee, a buttery warm croissant that came apart richly like taffy, and a pot of jam; and the strong morning breeze that had brought down small, green coconuts from the trees during the night, that dotted the white dew-damp beach in the early morning freshness, an island morning where the town was still asleep but the wind was already blowing hard and an old man with a rusty shopping cart was walking slowly along the strand collecting the fallen coconuts.

There were boats in the harbor from many places, most new, some older, and I saw a small, white schooner with the same traditional lines, same hull and color and appearance but for her rig, as my antique wooden gaff yawl, and it reminded me of her, at that moment propped up under cover in my back yard more than six hundred miles away. I felt a twinge of guilt and homesickness; I wished at that moment that I was looking at my own boat in the harbor. "One day I will sail you here," I said, inaudibly, more a thought than an utterance, speaking to my boat far and away across the expanse of sea.

When the sun ascended above the hillsides, now white and full of the strength of day, it shone upon impossibly bright turquoise waters, clear and reminiscent of an Olympic swimming pool, but with a misty, cloudy haziness that reminded one that it was salt water, not fresh. The gale was blowing hard but we were now secure to the commercial wharf in St. George's and the day was ours, at least while we remained.

Walking the streets; winding, hilly, cobblestoned, everywhere stone, brick, stucco, painted. A little like a part of Southern California, but quaint and colonial, English colonial, not Spanish. From a hilltop, I had sweeping views of the harbors and islets and the great sea beyond, from horizon to horizon a carpet of flat and everlasting blue. This place does not belong to the land, I noted to myself.

November-cool in Bermuda. Cloudy skies and sweater weather; I longed to spend a week inside one of those cozy, stone and stucco, antique cottages of St. George's, reposing on a carpet in front of an old fireplace before a smouldering palm log fire, sipping a rum or brandy. But then the sun blazed brilliant and dazzling white on the terracotta and white plastered rooftops, under clear, blue skies, and it was time to explore. Somehow my legs found energy, driven by my relentless curiosity that even fatigue could not quell, and we were all off in different directions while the Captain worked on repairs to some system or other belowdecks and then slept a few hours in the private quietude of the empty vessel.

I saw lush greenery everywhere; broad leaves, succulents, banana plants; yet the island is not quite tropical, and not quite temperate. Bermuda is a place in-between many things – between continents, barely above the surface of the sea, an annoyance perhaps to the ocean, and a place with a nearly perfect year-round temperature.

What would it be like if all the water were drained out of the ocean? A city or settlement on a mountaintop? The Parthenon and the Acropolis hilltop came to mind. No, more than that. The sea floor a few miles from Bermuda is nearly 4,000 meters down – more than 13,000 feet deep – the approximate height of much of Tenmile Range in the Rocky Mountains.

That evening, I took a bus into town with my fellow crewman, Andy. While we waited for the bus, the sky began to thunder, and then there was wind, lightning, and torrential rain. We stood under the bus stop awning and watched the little stream running down the hilly street turn into a brook. But then it was over and we were on our way to Hamilton, ending up at an English-style pub named the Hog Penny.

In the morning, we prepared the boat for departure, and took one last meal ashore, Sunday brunch, at the Wahoo restaurant, where I had a fine serving of poached salt codfish with a tomato relish, banana, and hard-boiled eggs. I looked out upon the harbor and watched the boats riding peacefully at anchor, and thought about the turbulent sea ahead, the return to discomfort and routine, and a part of me wished I could stay while another part of my heart knew that I had to go. In the end, there is no safety in staying anywhere, only stagnation and the gnawing uneasiness of not knowing. Life, I thought, is a passage, a transit punctuated by waypoints and occasional landfalls. But there is no salvation in abandoning the voyage; that is an illusion, because the voyage that is life continues relentlessly. All one loses is time in delay, and self-denial of vistas and experiences lost or postponed. We become soft through inactivity, without the struggle to temper our spirits, just as fire hardens a wooden spear-point. We lose our nerve and our spirit if we stay behind and hide amongst the palm fronds and succulent leaves in the cool, dark damp of the garden.

Out on the harbor, the sun-dappled wavelets raised by the freshening breeze sparkled brilliantly, like blinding diamonds, reflecting into my eyes; boats at anchor became silhouettes on a canvas of moving, fiery bold-brush dots of light and color thickly applied by an impressionist painter. Words of Scripture came to mind, even though misapplied: "For whoever would save his life, shall lose it." There was no staying behind; it was time to move on, to set sail, and to head south to the tropics.

◆◆◆◆◆◆◆

PRIVATEER Comes Home

As I drove along the winding, narrow road that edged ever closer to the Eastern Shore, I constantly scanned and scoured the land with my gaze, looking for my old boat, thinking that it would stand out against the background, jump out against the greenery in such a way that she could not be missed. I was filled with anxiety and apprehension. She would call out to me in some way, I though naively. I had been many hours in the truck now and although my body was stiff from the long ride, I felt nervously energized.

I had been told by the marina owner over the phone that my old boat was in poor condition, weathered, going to hell. I remember that first phone call from him, and felt my heart sink within me as I listened; yet hungry as I was for details, there were few. He was not a man of many words or florid description, as many working watermen of Maryland's Eastern Shore, who have a surprisingly great deal in common with Maine Yankees, are not. Yet it was just such a clinical, detailed description that I yearned for. My old gaff yawl that I had sold had been abandoned three years earlier by its new owner, after only one season in the water, left up on the hard at a small marina in a town called Rock Hall on the tranquil, sleepy western side of the Chesapeake. It was a long way from her former home in Rhode Island waters, and even further from the cold waters of Thomaston, Maine, where she had been built and launched in 1931.

Now I drove past lovely green fields of corn and soybeans, tin-roofed farmhouses and barns, occasionally glimpsing the water of the bay, now here a boat, now there a boat, a yacht club, a little marina. Almost there, I though, nearly eight hours and 400 miles after leaving my home early that morning. The yard owner was going to auction her off, or cut her up for scrap value to pay off the accumulated storage fees that the new owner had never paid. I had the opportunity, now, to reclaim her, nearly four years after I had sold her to a fellow who loved her but had simply bitten off more than he could chew. It is not an uncommon thing. But he had simply walked away from her, and left her to rot, and I felt angry about that.

I had been out in my garden, tending my tomatoes and planting Indian corn when Denise received an odd phone call from a stranger. "You'd better take this," she called to me. "It's from a boatyard in Maryland. It's about Privateer. The man says that he found your name and address in some old papers aboard the boat. He hasn't been able to reach – what was that guy's name – who you sold the boat to." I brushed the soft crumbly loam from my hands.

Oddly enough, I'd had dreams about the boat recently. I have always dreamed about my boats after I have parted company with them, for some inexplicable reason. The first big boat that I rebuilt and restored with much sweat, treasure, and time was a twin-screw wooden motorboat from the 1950s. After I sold it, and then years later after she was abandoned by the owner and broken up by the yard where he had left her, I began having dreams about her. In some of the dreams she was mine and whole again, and I was cruising with her, sometimes on familiar waters, sometimes far out in strange places that I had never seen. Perhaps that is a glimpse of the land and seascape of heaven, for people and for boats, where we all go to cruise when we die. Sometimes, in the dreams, the old cruiser would be apart, her hull open, disconnected wiring and engine parts everywhere, but she was mine again to restore and rebuild, almost a hopeless case, with many things missing, but I was undaunted and ready to begin work, if only I could remember how to do it all, all over again.

In my latest dream about Privateer, I was on the foredeck, she was at sea and under way, and I was bringing her home, and she was mine again. She had not been well cared for, but she was not really in bad shape at all. A friend was towing me, and I cleated the tow-line on the bitts and exclaimed how solid the deck was, and that she would surely come through it all right; she had been well-built, and no one could ruin her, especially now that she was back in the hands of her master. I am still strong enough, I thought, though more than fourteen years older than when I first received her; but I still know how to use my tools, adz and axe, chisel and saw, mallet and hammer; I will prevail. It was a strange, vivid dream, and when I awoke, it was still darkest night, in the wee hours of the morning before sunrise, and I lay on my back for awhile thinking about the dream, looking for meaning, and remembering, oddly, the a certain chapter in Joshua Slocum's Sailing Alone Around the World. It described a night where Captain Slocum was gravely ill, in a swoon from eating bad cheese and plums, while the Spray rode out a storm on the open sea. In his delirium, Slocum thinks that he is dockside and that careless draymen are tossing skiffs onto the Spray's deck, when in actuality they are seas breaking over his little vessel. But he calls out, daring the perpetrators to do their worst; "You cannot hurt the Spray," Slocum cries. "She is strong!" Mine was a prophetic dream, I guessed; strong dreams often are, even if their meanings are, at the time, utterly obscure. But this one made me uneasy and I could not go back to sleep again until after the gray first light of dawn had begun to filter through the window blinds.

Now at last I drove across the white crushed stone of the marina and past the tidy office buildings, storage sheds, and shower stalls to the back lot where a sad lot of boats stood, in the high season, up on poppets, high up on a bank overlooking the muddy Chester River. I saw my boat up on stands too, still and patient and waiting for me, looking in form like she always did, as though she had been in my backyard only yesterday, such was the overwhelming rush of familiarity. I pulled up to the end of the driveway, got out of the truck and just stood there, looking at her from a little distance, feeling waves of emotion rising up within me, which took all of my will to keep down lest they should rise unchecked, pour forth and flood over all.

Her paint was faded and the colors washed out and run together, oxidized and weathered by the hot Maryland sun, and she looked much like a pastel inexpertly smudged, or a watercolor blended and faded from being showered by rain or tears. Yet her high prow pointed out over the water, her bowsprit was still in place, and she looked proud and defiant, no hint of surrender, not asking for pity, no blame, no assignation of guilt, with all the quiet dignity and patience that only an inanimate object can have. These other things, after all, we assign to, or impose upon, ourselves. And as I stood there in the shimmering heat of the summer afternoon, not yet approaching, eyeing her from a distance, as firmly as she was propped up on the ground, she began to pitch and swim again in my sight as feelings welled up within me; it was as though she were out on the sea again. I walked over to my old boat and rested my hand on her solid rudder. "You are going home," I said.

A rickety ladder nearby allowed me to climb aboard. The cabin was a mess; mud wasps had entered through an open port and built little ugly nests in odd places, but it was a small port so not much else had come in. "There is much work to do," I heard myself saying, to myself and to the boat. It was terribly hot in the close cabin, and soon I was soaked with perspiration. But I knew all would be well, now. I had come to set in motion that which would bring my boat home again and fate full circle. He had not been able to destroy her, through neglect. Like Spray, my Privateer was strong. Paint was sadly peeling inside; but her sails were there, her fenders and lines and cushions and, remarkably, virtually everything else, from parrel beads to blocks, even her sweet bronze bell. The electrical panel had been partially disassembled; a new alternator was mounted on the engine. "He did something else wrong," I muttered. I'd heard, after he took the boat down to the Chesapeake that he had broken the mizzen gaff, or boom. These were missing, nowhere to be seen. "But I can make new spars," I said aloud, to myself, and perhaps to the boat, reassuringly.

I realized, then, from the way that I felt inside, that this was, and is, more than just a boat; I had not realized it until after she had been sold, and was gone. Why? Perhaps it is the work that must go into restoring a boat, and then realizing the dream of sailing her. Maybe it is because each time we are cut or injured working the wood, and spill a little blood, we realize that the cost is now complete; one has given in all ways. Perhaps we begin to identify with the boat, and with each screw driven, each plank refastened, a part of ourselves becomes bonded as to the frames.

This is why I will say, and warn others, about a lesson sorely learned, but perhaps not learned too late, that you must never, ever sell, or willingly relinquish, anything to which a part of your soul is inseparably bound. If you do so, you will hunger to retrieve it ever afterward, until it is restored to you. Sometimes, our lives and the fate of things, as well as other people, are inexplicably intertwined. When they are no longer apart, both become whole again.

So I closed her up and went to the marina office to meet the yard owner, to write a check, to secure her release, and complete the tedious pages of paperwork, and to arrange trucking, since she was not in proper condition for a sea-journey of hundreds of miles. It would take every resource that I had, but that did not concern me; for this was the pearl of great price; and I was ready to sell all that I had in order to obtain her.

I stayed overnight in Rock Hall that evening, at a neat little motor lodge down by the harbor, and listened to a band play Jimmy Buffett tunes on the dock next to the Waterman's Crab House

Restaurant. There was an outdoor bar, with a big crowd of friendly locals, and I drank too much cool beer while I daydreamed and watched the many boats coming in off the placid Chesapeake. Their red and green running lights glowed in the gathering dusk as they pushed gentle bow-waves through the shimmering water that reflected the golden yellow glow of shoreside lights across the narrow river entrance. The moon was rising over the bay and the night was warm and pleasant. I saw Doug, the marina owner, at the bar with his wife and friends, and he kindly bought me a drink and paid me a compliment. I saw him speak to his wife, and I knew that he was telling her that I was the one who had come to take the boat home and fix her up.

Later, before I went back to my room to sleep, I walked down to a quiet place on the pier, and felt at peace, connected to my past, my memories of many things flowing together in a steady current down the years of my life like the brackish river flowing seaward beneath my feet. All was in motion again, headed for the open water, and I felt happy to have a part of myself back.

◆◆◆◆◆◆◆

Last Trip of the Season

The boating season seems to end earlier up on Massachusetts' North Shore than it does in waters farther south. The water is colder up there, above the Cape, (Both Cod and Ann), and the cold coast of Maine practically breathes down upon the short New Hampshire shoreline and coast around the mouth of the Merrimack.

So, sadly enough, one early November, my friend Captain Jon decided that it was time to take his little double-ended diesel power boat – no more than 20-something-foot vessel, formerly a freighter's lifeboat, the *Sea Hagy* (pronounced *haggie* – the spelling is Jon's) – from her seasonal marina berth in the Merrimack River, just up a couple of miles in Amesbury, Mass., to haul out at a boatyard in Hampton, N.H., in the Hampton River a few miles away. To get there, they must exit the river and go on the "outside" – Massachusetts Bay, open water – before heading into the Hampton River inlet. The weather can be tricky and changeable this late in the season and the river mouths have strong currents since the tidal changes are greater. Our rough-and-ready friend Captain Bob was happy to help out and to accompany him.

A few years back, Jon paid an older local retired fellow to rebuild his boat and put a nice cabin on it, etc., as Jon had come into a little inheritance money. The man had done some boatbuilding up on the Newbury waterfront for many years and knew his trade. He designed a neat cabin with round ports, a rather Popeye-ish look to it, and Jon rechristened the *Sea Hagy* (from the sea hag in the early Popeye cartoons – and I once heard him refer to a former girlfriend that way) and launched her into the Merrimack once again. The fellow who did the months of refurbishment died soon afterwards, but that was unrelated.

Captain Jon has been my friend for many years. He is a gentle giant of a fellow, a true salty North Shore Yankee who has always been fascinated by treasure and pirates. If called to be a pirate, however, he would be too compassionate to make even a mouse walk the plank. He is very good at collecting things that other people no longer have any use for, to the great chagrin of his neighbors, and can make do with many things that other folks would have long ago consigned to the dump, which, of course, is where Jon finds many of his treasures. He is also a handy fellow around the house, but not always around boats.

The first time I went aboard *Sea Hagy*, I was nearly tripped up in the rat's nest of tangled lines on the foredeck. "Jon!" I exclaimed, "You need to coil these things – and then stow most of them!" Another time, he could not leave the dock because, for some inexplicable reason, the single propeller had contrived to fall off, and was sitting in the mud beneath the keel at the slip. Jon's friend Captain Bob knew how to dive without swallowing too much water, and for the price of a shot of whisky and a couple of beers, he retrieved the propeller, but the *Hagy* had to be hauled for an hour to re-attach the three-bladed prop.

So now we move ahead to the little trip around to the Hampton River, with both skippers aboard, and the old blue Perkins four-cylinder growling to life at the slip in Amesbury. I have said enough; it is time for Captain Jon to pick up the narrative, just as he related it to me some months ago:

"Captain Bob and I checked the NOAA forecast and the weather was to be cold and clear with waves less than two feet, so we pondered taking the boat around from the Merrimack River to the Hampton River. Only around four or five nautical miles, says Bob, and I say it is time we make the voyage because we were literally running out of dockage in the river. They started hauling dock on October 15 and we had to move from that 'country club' that has so many rules that I wonder why I went there in the first place. Didn't use the swimming pool once and that was a crime. They got a little put out with me in the summer when I left some bait slated for my traps on the boat." (Capt. Jon fancies himself a gentleman lobsterman – he keeps a few traps, and bought a quantity of smelly bait which he neglected to remove from the marina when he went off to Florida for a week in the unseasonably-warm last weeks in October).

"I had that bait in a nice cooler, but as the sun started to beat down on the cooler it must have created some fumes or gas as the bait fish started to expand and lifted the cover up enough so the contents sort of created a haze around the Sea Hagy and by afternoon a zephyr started blowing in the general direction of the club house. As the day wore on, the bait cooler started to stink something awful and it kind of put a damper on some special party or dance that was happening early evening. They had some city dignitaries over giving speeches and rubbing elbows with the Mucky Mucks. By suppertime there was such a foul smell coming off the

15

docks that I got a call from the Commodore ordering me to do something about it. Of course I was on vacation and really couldn't do much from a distance, so I called Captain Bob and he went down with the old Dodge pickup truck and fetched the bait from the farthest corner of the boat yard where it had been removed by one of the dock hands. When Bob arrived, the cooler had been neatly wrapped with three layers of heavy plastic bags.

Commodore had enough time to pull away from the festivities and started giving Captain Bob quite a tongue lashing, stating rules and regulations and such, but Bob would have none of it; he replied with a comment about the rules and regulations being about as smelly as the fish, and that anyway, he was just the messenger."

"As I said earlier, on the day of the trip, after I had returned from my travels, Bob had sworn that he had looked at the weather report, and that it seemed like clear sailing, so we fetched the water bottles and antifreeze and went down to the dock to start up the engine. It was sunny, but it was a cold day and when we got to the old Hat Factory in Amesbury where the *Sea Hagy* was slipped, it looked kind of lonely out there being the next to last boat on the floating dock. There was no ramp left for us to get on to the main dock. They had removed it. So we pondered a bit and pretty soon Dan the jovial dock master came by with his workboat and we hitched a ride over to the Hag. We boarded her and I opened up the hatch and gave her a fresh drink of antifreeze, turned on the blower, set the throttle, and cranked over the *Sea Hagy's* old blue Perkins. She caught on the second round of cranking and that old workhorse sprang to life. After a couple of minutes she was purring like a kitten, so we said our hasty good-byes to Dan and thanked him for his kindness. He said it was a good thing we were both going out together 'cause it was cold and the mouth of the river was unforgiving this time of year.

We left Dan standing on the dock as we made a port turn out of the Marina and headed downriver. It was a spectacular day with some of the reds and yellows still showing on the trees. We went past the bridge where Grampa Patten (Capt. Jon's famous maternal grandpa) jumped off the bridge when younger and got his head stuck in the mud. The old church with its white steeple and Lowell's boat yard all reflecting in the water of the Merrimack as we passed Amesbury was quite a pretty sight. The *Sea Hagy* had the river to herself and with an outgoing tide we were plowing along at about six and a half knots. It was exhilarating watching the water rush by the bow. All was good until we made nun number two beyond the spindle and about opposite black rocks. The weather turned a fowl (sic) gray with a nasty looking squall line coming out of the Northwest. In the fifteen or twenty minutes that it took us to get to that point the wind had risen about 15 knots and whitecaps were popping up in the harbor.

I said to Bob, "It looks like a squall" and just as I pondered that we got hit with a gust of wind and snow flurries that shivered me timbers. It was snowing and sleeting sideways and we could make out that the seas were rising at the mouth, but on we drove into it. We came around the north jetty doing seven knots and were immediately greeted with four-footers building. I told Bob that we might ride it out if we could get in a little closer to the beach, which was a windward shore, but the wind climbed another 10 knots and it was getting downright snotty off Salisbury Beach."

"Finally, I managed to get the *Hagy* turned around and headed in toward the mouth of the Hampton River. The waves were building and that squall just seemed to hang around the mouth for the longest time. As we turned with great caution, the old *Hag* almost got upended and her fog bell came out of its bracket and fell onto the deck with a loud 'clang'. Hold on says I, as there's a steep one coming. Over the bar a large wave reared up and picked up our good vessel like a piece of driftwood. But the tide was incoming against the wind, with a sizable swell from the east, and even though the waves were steep, we were able to surf down them into the river, under the bridge, and into calmer water as the wind dropped down and the squalls of snow flurries began to slow. The Sea Hag slithered up into the harbor's protected waters, and then as quick as the squall blew in, it was gone, leaving the waters angry behind her. Bob looked over toward Hampton Marsh to the west, and saw the golden, late-afternoon sun poking its head out from under the clouds that were clearing from that direction. We turned about just then we saw the most beautiful rainbow off to the east, where the squall had gone. Captain Bob called it a snow-bow, as there were snow flurries all about, and these had made the bow. Two harbor seals surfaced at that time, and the wonderment of that made the conclusion of the trip all that more enjoyable."

"When we got to the slip, we tied her up, put the fenders along-side so all was snug, and then went up the dock to the old tavern on route One-A and had a little whisky snorter to toast the trip before heading home."

♦♦♦♦♦♦♦

Men of the Sea

Santiago, Hemingway's old fisherman, wisely reminds us that young lads sleep late and hard. It's true; having once been a young boy, and later a father, I can attest that the only reasons a young boy will get up out of bed in the middle of the night are either to visit the bathroom, or worse, to throw up all over the hallway on the way to the bathroom, thanks to the nasty little stomach-virus he picked up at school the previous day. Oh, and there is one other reason – the prospect of going on an early-morning boat-ride with Grandpa in Uncle George's new Luhrs power cruiser. Otherwise, most boys, if not all, never willingly get out of bed before sunrise.

Many years ago, my Uncle George bought a Luhrs powerboat. It was wooden, lap-strake planked, twenty-something feet long, with a clipper bow and a single inboard engine, a Chrysler Crown, the old flathead six-cylinder type. It wasn't new, but it was in very nice shape. It was located at the old Tripp's boatyard in the Westport River, across the little harbor from the fishing docks at Westport Point, Massachusetts. Uncle George and his dad, my Grandpa, planned to bring the boat from Tripp's to Grandpa's Bristol, R.I., mooring in Bristol Harbor one Saturday morning in early September. George's son, Dan, and I were invited along for the cruise. Dan was almost my age – a year younger – and we were used to spending a lot of time together in Grandpa's boats.

Dan was a chubby kid with blond crew-cut hair and he looked a little like the 'bad boy' cartoon decal that one occasionally sees on large pickup trucks, an image of a naughty lad relieving himself someplace where he ought not to be doing so. Dan had a bit of a mean streak in him, but that normally didn't bother me and both Dan and I had twelve-foot wooden skiffs that Grandpa had built for us and kept on the dinghy floats down at the Bristol Yacht Club. Grandpa also had a gaff beetle cat that we had each learned to sail. Thanks to Grandpa's boatbuilding and woodworking skills, the old Beetle Cat, which bore a heavy, multi-layer coating of Kirby's green paint, never leaked a drop. Dan used to always try to run over people's mooring floats, or swamp the boat when we were sailing together, usually out in the middle of Bristol harbor, but because a Beetle cat is so difficult to capsize due to its width, Dan never suc-ceeded, which is probably why I am here now to write this story.

And although we spent a lot of time together in small boats, we were excited because we knew that this day would be different from the others. We were going for a ride in a big power boat, and the prospect of a daylong trip across distant waters was exciting, especially since we would be going with the men! This made us feel special, important in a way, just a little more grown up, perhaps, than we really were.

Grandpa's plan was to leave Bristol for Westport well before dawn, to get an early start on the day. It was fall now, Grandpa said, and the weather out on Buzzard's Bay and off Sakonnet Point could be changeable. Grandpa said that it could get rough later in the day, so it was wisest to leave early, riding together in the old Ford Country Squire station wagon. I don't remember if Grandma rode with us, in order to drive the car home after we had left the dock, since we would not be coming back to Tripp's; but she probably did.

Dan and I slept over at Grandpa and Grandma's house that night. Of course, we were excited, and stayed up late talking; Grandma knocked on the bedroom door once, and scolded us, telling us that it was time to be quiet and get to sleep; when that didn't work, finally, Grandpa came upstairs and sternly told us that we must pipe down and go to sleep because we would be rising very early, and if we didn't go to sleep very soon, we would not be allowed to go at all!

Well, of course, that stern admonition worked; the light went out, and we each tried very hard to go to sleep, which, due to the lateness of the hour, came along naturally all by itself. But as I drifted off, the tantalizing aroma of chourico and peppers cooking reached my nostrils and made my belly grumble. Downstairs in the kitchen, Grandma was making tomorrow's lunch for the boat ride.

Chourico is a red, spicy, delicious Portuguese sausage. As one who grew up in Rhode Island and nearby Southeastern Massachusetts, I can say that Portuguese people were my neighbors, schoolmates, and friends; their cuisine had become so well blended into mainstream New England cooking that one did not even think twice about it; my Irish-ethnic Grandma could whip up a batch of chourico and peppers as convincingly as any Portuguese lady in Bristol; and furthermore, of all the things one may stuff into a sub-roll or torpedo sandwich roll, few things are more satisfying, appetizing, or tasty as chourico and peppers.

Grandma would slice up the chourico and fry it in a black-iron skillet in a little olive oil with chopped green bell peppers, onions, and garlic; then she would add some Portuguese red crushed pepper, tomato paste, and a few other unknown enhancements ("a little this and that," she would say) to make a thick saucy filling, which would then be stuffed into the top of a torpedo roll, in similar fashion to a meatball sandwich, and served hot.

I don't remember waking up that morning in the pre-dawn darkness; Grandpa had a gentle way of waking us by touching one foot and wiggling it a little bit until we woke up – and because we were too young to be allowed coffee, that was an adult drink, Grandma served us tea – she had boiled the kettle before we had been awakened. The aroma of re-heated chourico and peppers filled the house. She had re-warmed the skillet so that the mixture was piping hot, and then filled nearly a dozen torpedo rolls with the spicy filling, and wrapped each sandwich individually in waxed paper. Then, she had packed them snugly into an old, round, potato-chip bin. I remember it well; it was a sturdy, cylindrical container, much resembling a hat box, with red printing on it – an image of a housewife and the words "Made-Rite Potato Chips" printed on the side. Even though the potato chips were long gone, it was such a handy and durable container that it was perfect to pack a bunch of chourico and pepper sandwiches in. Grandma pressed the lid firmly in place; I lifted it, and it seemed heavy, and just slightly warm, with the aroma of the sandwiches barely seeping through.

Grandpa brought the old galvanized steel Coca-cola cooler up from the cellar. It had an aluminum upper tray in it and was painted red, with the Coca-Cola logo script in white lettering on the sides. It was all metal, old-style, heavy, with a drain spigot on the bottom and a handle on top that snapped closed over the lid and held the lid shut. It would keep things cold for a very long time when Grandpa put a piece of block ice in it, and the rugged cooler was a necessary companion on all boat trips and picnics. Grandpa put the water jug into the cooler with a bunch of large ice cubes from the freezer, and some bottles of Fanta soda (in Massachusetts they still call it tonic) and in particular a few bottles of orange Fanta, because Grandpa knew that I liked orange Fanta especially.

We left in the darkness, but once the car was moving, I could see the blue of the lightening sky to the east, toward Fall River. The lights of the city still twinkled out of the black mass of the land as we crossed the Taunton River on the old Brightman Street Bridge and drove up along Route 6 through the city. It had become fairly light – and both Dan and I were yawning – when we passed east of Fall River and into Westport, wending our way in the gathering dawn along the winding road to Tripp's that passed by Horseneck Beach. Little scrubby pitchpines lined the dune-like landscape that flanked the road, and the high tree-covered dunes along the shore loomed high above us and hid our view of the sea.

An old wooden freight barge, massive-timbered like a great old sailing ship, had been beached next to Tripp's dock and although it was half sunk, the part of it above water at high tide was used as a dinghy storage dock, and support for the dock and float framework. Tired now and open to the sea, it had become a permanent part of the marina's pier system, but to me it seemed ancient, a relic of bygone times. As the golden sun peeked through the still-leafy treetops and began to beam down on the still harbor lined with bright-green spears of eelgrass, I climbed out onto the old barge and looked down through a hole in the deck while Grandpa and Uncle George were busy getting the boat ready. Through the hole I peered into a dark cavern illuminated by shafts of sunlight from the outside, filling the great dark void with an eerie golden-green glow. Through the semi-transparent, deep water, I glimpsed the massive sunken skeleton-timbers of the barge, the side planking long gone, the great square frames reaching down and disappearing into the lime-green depths of the harbor to an unseen bottom way below. It was high tide. This scary, fantastic back-lit vision of the deep, heavy with shadow and seaweed, fired my imagination; it could have been a vision of the hundreds of wrecks of centuries of wooden ships in the lost mire of the Sargasso Sea. But it was a short–lived vision.

"Hey, get out of there!" Grandpa's angry voice called out. "You'll get hurt over there! You're not supposed to be climbing on that!"

Dan was in the boat, sitting on the engine-box pretending to be a good boy, smirking at me with an air of 'ha, ha, you got in trouble. Bleeaahhhh.' He had one up on me – ever so slightly – and he savored the morsel, small as it was.

Now the engine had been started and it grumbled and rumbled with a deep-throated voice and belched clouds of white exhaust and steam while the water coughed and burbled around the exhaust pipe just below the waterline off the transom. I could smell the odd old marine gasoline engine exhaust smell – not especially unpleasant – as we backed out of the slip. The engine had warmed up, and was ticking and purring, the way the old flathead engines used to, click-ety-smooth like a big sewing machine, and then commenced to roar in its authoritative way as Grandpa throttled up and we powered out into the channel toward the river mouth. The water boiled behind us and big clouds of misty exhaust poured out behind into the cool air and as quickly disappeared into nothingness as they drifted astern. Dan and I went below to explore the main cabin; there was not much more than a vee-shaped room with a berth on either side, and what looked like a cramped closet with a funny-looking little toilet in it. We lay down on the berth cushions for a few moments, just to try them out, imagining that we were on a long sea voyage; but we were too excited to remain in them for very long, and soon we were back on deck.

I remember one particular image, still alive in my mind after all these years, of exiting the river mouth and heading out onto Buzzard's Bay in the cool morning, the sea mirror-calm, and the sky a lovely blue with horizontal steaks of mauve stretching away across the southern horizon. I thought that I never would have imagined that early morning at sea could be so beautiful. Directly ahead lay the sad, rust-colored wreckage of the old cement barge on Hen and Chickens shoal – Grandpa told us the story of it, how an old tug and barge of cement had gone aground on the rocks during a hurricane in the 1940s – and added quickly that "we weren't going over there," which disappointed me slightly, because although the visible wreck was a fearsome thing, my young boy's curiosity drove me to want to see the wreck anyway.

Picture it now, if you will; we are heading out into Buzzard's Bay; the sandy shoreline and green land beyond, the high dunes of Westport Point, and the gray roofs of Acoaxet recede into the dis-tance behind us as we glide out across the vast expanse of the bay. The island of Cuttyhunk rises above the sea to the left, but does not close; we are not going there, either. Somewhere in the distance, off toward the endless ocean to the southwest, there is a plume of dark smoke; it rises and rises, as if surfacing like a great whale out of the sea, to gradually reveal the wheelhouse, high prow, and low hull of a big brick-red ocean-going tugboat and towed barge well behind it, laboring up the bay toward the Cape Cod Canal. We will stay out of his way. The water around the boat is clean, aqua-blue, with a white foamy wake trailing astern; Grandpa and Uncle George are taking turns at the helm, behind the windshield, talking, but Dan and I cannot hear much of what they say. Grandpa lights his pipe, and the aroma of toasted vanilla Cavendish floats back to Dan and I; that is the aroma that we always associate with Grandpa.

Halfway to the strange, rugged rock-island boulders of Sakonnet Point, our stomachs are growling again; salt water and sea air do marvelous things for one's appetite, especially for the appetite of a boy. I have been thinking about the sandwiches in the potato chip drum; the red-inked smiling image of the lady with a pearl necklace, printed on the outside, is happily calling me to lunch, I imagine. Perhaps we are all thinking the same thing; Grandpa opens the lid and distributes the chourico and pepper sandwiches. They are still warm! I eat quickly – one, then two – thinking that I have never tasted anything so wonderfully delicious in my life, washed down with an orange Fanta. Normally chatty Dan is unusually quiet; his porky face seems to be actually enveloping his sandwich, like a starfish's stomach around its prey, or folding around it the way a tree slowly absorbs a metal sign that has been nailed to it for too many years; or even the way a baseball might sink into a soft loaf of risen bread dough if dropped into the middle of it. I am still at the end of my first sandwich when he has already finished his second. He wants my second sandwich; I say no, and we start to fight. Grandpa turns around.

"Hey you guys, cut that out! Get along with each other!" Dan looks like he is going to pout; his lower lip puffs out and forms an arch.

When we are done eating, there is red tomato sauce smeared all around our mouths, and Grandpa gives us soft paper napkins to wipe our faces clean.

Our trip took us around Sakonnet Point, up the Sakonnet River, and into Mount Hope Bay. As we passed under the century-old derelict swinging railroad bridge in Tiverton – since torn down – Grandpa told us about Great-grandpa McGrath, Grandma's dad, and how, as a young man, he was an engineer on a steam locomotive that used to cross that bridge, back in the 1900s when he worked for the Old Colony Railroad. Fishermen with dark faces, Cape Verdean men from Fall River, are fishing from the bridge. They smile, and wave to us as we pass; the four of us wave back.

We turn at Common Fence Point, and head southwest, to round Bristol Neck; passing under the Mount Hope Bridge, now, we are heading for Bristol Harbor; it is early afternoon, and the wind has sprung up brisk and cool out of the northwest. Little whitecaps scud across a lightly choppy Narragansett Bay; puffy, fluffy white cottony cumulus clouds are frolicking across the deep blue September sky. We tie up to the dock, and step off – Dan and I – feeling like the greatest seamen who ever lived. That night, as I fall asleep, the bed will move, seemingly, ever so slightly, like the deck of the boat, rocking me to sleep with unforgettable sensations and images of our grand seagoing adventure that, like the enduring love for a Grandfather and Grandmother remembered, will never diminish nor fade from the unclouded crystal spyglass-lens of mind and heart.

◆◆◆◆◆◆◆

Sailing to Paradise

A late-season voyage aboard the vintage 1926 Herreshoff
staysail schooner Mary Rose from Rhode Island to Tortola, BVI

On Monday, November 22, 2010, the beginning of Thanksgiving week, a crew of four men from southern New England set out from Portsmouth, R.I., aboard the vintage 1926 Herreshoff staysail schooner *Mary Rose*. Our destination was the island of Tortola, in the British Virgin Islands. We sailed her down there to fulfill her owner's desire to have her spend the winter down in that tropical paradise, but it was a voyage that almost didn't happen.

She had only been re-launched a few weeks before, at the Hinckley dock in Little Harbor, Portsmouth, after a major refit following disastrous damage caused by her breaking loose and running up on the rocks a year or two before. Holes had been knocked into her hull that a man could walk through without bending his neck. But she had been carefully restored and robustly repaired, her double-planked topsides rebuilt and some of her steel frames – composite construction for 1926 – replaced. She wet her keel once more without a hitch on a fine, mild, Indian-Summer day in late October, and had motored to Bristol to moor at the Herreshoff Museum dock.

A couple of weeks later, in a northerly blow on November 8, the 29-ton, 65-foot (on deck) wooden schooner broke free of her mooring in front of Herreshoff's and drifted aground and ashore at Love Rocks, Captain Nat Herreshoff's old estate, where, miraculously, she wedged her keel gently between two ledges and remained upright, and was refloated at the following high tide. She was towed back to Portsmouth and hauled, only to show that the gentle hand that had guided her into that slot – with her bowsprit practically reaching the lawn of her designer's old homestead – had done so with care; she had not suffered a scratch! And although some may consider her grounding a bad omen, I regarded her escape, unscathed, as a good one, although the news of it on that wind-whipped morning had scared the dickens out of me; I was certain that the voyage was finished before it had begun.

But it had not, and we left on a cold, gray Monday, and despite the cold, we were cheerful, with buoyant spirits, happy to be heading to sea, knowing that we were embarking on an adventure of perhaps two weeks, hoping for the best, but mentally prepared for what might be a rough trip. Why did I go? I went because it was an opportunity for adventure, to recharge my batteries, so to speak; to test myself mentally and physically. The other reason was to gain more valuable sea-time and practically work on watch-standing, steering, navigation, chart reading and plotting, radio communications, sailing, weather interpretation, clouds, forecasting, and much more. As a licensed Captain, it is important for me to keep my skills sharp by keeping them in play, and retain that knowledge through use. What did I gain? On a personal level, I surprised myself with my ability to endure, and brought new and wonderful experiences and destinations into the portfolio of my life, experiences that were the best of all things – new, dangerous, and characterized by the sublime paradox of being both frightening and awesomely beautiful at the same time. No experience has such awe-inspiring power over a man's soul as the latter does, the paradox of 'terrifying beauty'.

The *Mary Rose's* skipper, Capt. Thomas Bradford, originally from Cape Cod, and a descendant of Pilgrim father William Bradford, knew her well. He had overseen her careful reconstruction and refitting. I signed on as Mate; together, the Captain and I were the old guys; then there were the two young men, Jason Baker, an able shipwright, IYRS trained, whose careful work on the *Mary Rose's* restoration would stand us in good stead during the rough weather ahead; and Andy Furlong, the 'Bo'sun', able sailor and the fellow who would stay behind in Tortola aboard the *Mary Rose* as her caretaker during the winter months.

Mary Rose is a unique lady. She's full-keel, draws nine feet, so she is hardly a warm-water boat; she's rather narrow, stable and quick to right herself, and although she was designed with a schooner rig, she has nothing in common with the classic image of a schooner such as the down-easters or even Alden schooners. No, put your hand over her sail plan, and what you are left with is the quick hull of a characteristic Herreshoff design. For my own opinion, I would say that *Mary Rose* is perhaps an example of the finest of Nat Herreshoff's prodigious genius. She is a performance cruiser with racing lines, designed for blue water, incorporating the best of both intentions, i.e., racing and cruising. In terms of performance, on a reach, close reach, or even windward beat, she moves like a racehorse; fast, smooth, capable, cutting through seas like a hot knife through butter, and she loves a capful of wind. But she is not happy with a wind directly behind, so the wind must come off the quarter, and she does not like a heavy sea off the quarter either. She rolls terribly in a quartering sea with not enough wind, or even when she has a moderate amount, and we had not been at sea too many days before we were referring to our ship as the *"Mary Rolls."*

We left late in the season, perhaps later than we should have, but there were many considerations that went into the departure date that are too numerous to list here, but suffice to say that we could not have departed earlier. As a consequence, we immediately encountered rough weather, 40-knot gales and 18-foot seas, which made the first week of our trip rough, wet, cold, and at times dangerous.

The night before we departed, a Sunday, the four of us, plus our wives, friends, and the younger fellows' lady friends, had met at Aidan's, our favorite Irish pub in Bristol, for a pre-departure party, food, pints of ale, and an evening of getting to know one another; it had been Captain Tom's idea. It was riotous fun; Hughie and Gerry Purcell, our long-time musician friends who are originally from Ireland, played fun and bawdy tunes, and the guitar and fiddle rang out. The spirit was infectious; energy ran high, and I felt charged down through the very core of my being. People who did not know us joined in the fun, danced, and spilled beer. Hughie sang "The Leaving of Liverpool" and substituted his own satirical lyrics to give Captain Tom and the rest of us a chuckle.

Captain Tom had divided us into two watches of six hours each, and six hours is a long watch especially in bad weather. Jason and I had the 6 a.m. – noon, and 6 pm – midnight watches every day; Captain Tom and Andy took the other two. This meant a full 12 hours each day on watch and on the helm for each of us, every day, albeit split up. *Mary Rose's* traditional cockpit offered no shelter from the weather whatsoever; rain, spray, wind, and cold were our enemies as well as our constant companions. There was no wheelhouse, no cockpit dodger, no awning, no Bimini. Only a small dodger covered the entrance to the companionway going below. There was no place to hide. We each took turns on watch hand-steering for two hours each, then standing by in the drenching cockpit trying to stay warm and stay awake. Our faces burned from the effects of driven spray, salt and wind; it was as though they were badly sunburned, and the skin felt hot and angry when we went below and even touched it with a damp wash-cloth. We each wore layers of wool and polar fleece, covered by foul weather rain gear, and wore inflatable life vests and harnesses in the cockpit at all times in rough weather. There were plenty of places to 'clip on', and we went nowhere on deck without being clipped to a pad-eye or a jack line.

Jason and Andy handled the foredeck work, at the Captain's direction; my specialty became the helm, keeping her controlled and steady while the young men did their dangerous work on the plunging, soaked foredeck managing the sails, fixing problems, reefing, whatever was needed. At night, we turned on the spreader lights to illuminate the deck, and it was a scene out of a wild, wet Hell in motion of deadly swinging spars and luffing sails on a pitching and careening deck, sails suddenly filling, snapping and booming like cannon-shots, surrounded by roaring darkness, wind, and blowing spray.

During the first week, sleep was nearly impossible in the rough seas. We all became terribly sleep deprived, so we tried to sleep whenever we could, whenever we were not on watch. Judgment became fuzzy, and all of us at one time or another hallucinated a little at night.

Fixed berths tilt, pitch, and yaw with the vessel, unlike hammocks; so in order to get to sleep, one must immobilize one's body. If your body moves or your head rolls, you will not sleep. So I packed nearly a dozen pillows and cushions of all kinds around my body, something akin to chocking the wheels of a truck, to immobilize myself. Then I had to learn to 'tune out' the creaking of the vessel, the slamming, hammering of her hull, seas washing aboard, cabinets emptying their contents onto the deck in the main cabin, and other loud noises. At one point, an entire cabinet of books blew open and spilled all over the cabin deck, where one of the young guys was sleeping. Another time, a heavy metal winch handle came happily dancing down the ladder from the charthouse enclosure above, making a racket but thankfully not gouging up the woodwork.

We got an early taste of what we were in for right after we left Newport, heading out on a strong, outflowing moon tide, into the teeth of an opposing southwesterly. I was on the helm, and Captain Tom, Jason, and Andy went forward to sort out a problem with the Yankee, our jib out on the bowsprit that is hanked onto the forestay. It was furled but was becoming undone and had to be secured before it got loose. This sail would cause us much grief several times during the voyage. All of a sudden, three impossibly steep waves at least ten feet high in quick succession brought the *Mary Rose* – all 65 feet of her – into an incredible up and down pitching, with the result that she plowed into the third wave and took green water over the bow. Captain Tom, who was up there at the time, disappeared under water for a second or two, and then emerged, saucer-eyed and not knowing whether or not he should be surprised, angry, or both; he was thoroughly drenched, dunked, and doused in November water, and the rest of us were completely astonished.

That first rough night, the full moon was rising; the sea was beautiful, and the wind brisk; the distant light of Gay Head, or Aquinnah, on Martha's Vineyard, beyond the horizon, flashed against the sky every few seconds. We occasionally saw the lights of fishing boats, headed in, from time to time, one of them presenting an eerie, phantasmic image as it steamed past a mile away, flocks of sea-birds circling around its stern, in and out of its bright lights like a swarm of fireflies as it passed. Out of the corner of my eye, off the port side of the *Mary Rose*, in the shimmering white path that led to the rising moon, I thought at one point that I saw something in the water, a black silhouette of a dorsal fin. I rubbed my eyes, and looked again; nothing. Then moments later, more black silhouettes, which I recognized as dolphins leaping and shooting like torpedoes through the waves, following us, staying alongside, one, then two, then a half dozen, keeping with us, companions on our trip. They cheered my heart; they reminded me again of Hemingway's *Old Man and the Sea*, where Santiago, far out at sea and alone in his fishing boat, notices the birds and other creatures and muses that no one is ever truly alone on the sea. The dolphins followed us from time to time, both day and at night, but after Bermuda, we never saw them again, nor did we see whales or much other wildlife except for the odd beauty of a white-tailed tropic bird, or so it is called, that hovered above our masts from time to time from the day that we left Bermuda. This strange but beautiful bird has a long, single tail extending out nearly the length of its body, like a kite-tail, and it reminded us that we were passing into a new and exotic climate as we wove our way south toward the promise of the tropics.

We sailed into the teeth of a roaring gale; it was not due to a low-pressure system, but rather a major cold front, a huge high-pressure system moving eastward from the continent and the dipping Jet Stream. So we had high winds, but no rain or stormy weather. Winds were 30 to 35 knots steady, gusting to 40, and one gust hit 49 knots. Big seas built up, and we could only hang on, try to sleep, steer the boat, keep hydrated, and try to stay warm. At night, the masts swayed wildly in the darkness beneath a sky brilliant with stars that instead of twinkling, remained cold, fixed points of light. The Milky Way glowed as a belt of light across the heavens; the wind howled and the seas roared as they broke alongside. The moon rose later each night as it waned from full, but it illuminated a wild ocean scene under a clear sky, a scene of foaming crests and silver hills rushing by as spray dashed over the foredeck and blew aft. Dolphins followed us, leaping out of the water at night by the moonlight, frolicking around the boat by day.

It was a rough week, rough without let-up, which stressed all of us both mentally and physically. One night, I began hallucinating, and I knew it. I'd had very little sleep for the past four days. I was at the helm steering *Mary Rose* on a southerly course under reduced sail as she fought her way through high seas and gale-force winds in the impenetrable blackness of a deeply overcast night. I had been guiding her with the help of two orange-amber-lit analog wind indicator dials. I had been staring at them for nearly three hours, keeping the *Mary Rose's* unseen sails full as we lunged ahead, slogging to windward.

Now, these two luminous dials with dark centers, crusted with salt and spattered with drops of sea-spray, had become two lovely orange-frosted doughnuts, and I could not get that image to change in my mind. It was true that I had eaten very little for several days and two luscious frosted doughnuts would have been heavenly, even at that moment. But the odd image inversion, much like what sometimes happens when viewing an aerial photograph, when the high and low features reverse in optical illusion, only made the dials harder to see, and I cursed. It was bad enough that I was wet and cold and constantly being drenched with chilling salt spray from seas breaking over the bow in the darkness, but I couldn't see a thing – neither the big seas, nor the sails, nor anything that was not illuminated. Yet I could feel her hull slam into a sea, and two seconds later, after just enough time for me to turn my head, I was doused as effectively as if someone had thrown a huge bucket of seawater at me from only a few feet away.

Of course, I was not the only one of the *Mary Rose's* four-man crew who had seen things. Andy, on his helm watch, had imagined a coil of rope to be our Captain Tom, sitting in the darkened cockpit hunched over, avoiding the spray, and began talking to him. Only when Captain Tom did not respond did he look closer to see that Tom had become a big coil of three-strand polyester, the main sheet, as it were. On another occasion, my watch-mate, Jason, thought he saw me in the cockpit at night, and spoke to me, and when I did not respond, he looked down and was startled to see that I was not there. I had actually gone below briefly, but he had not seen me leave, and was as alarmed as poor Andy was, in his weariness worrying that Captain Tom had accidentally fallen overboard, leaving only the coiled mainsheet in his stead.

The problem with cold weather is condensation under your oilskins or rain gear. It doesn't breathe, so even if your oilies keep the spray off of your clothing beneath, soon your perspiration and body moisture condenses on the inside surfaces and makes your clothes damp. They don't dry appreciably during your six hours off watch, so we slept in our clothes so that our body heat would help accelerate their drying before we had to go back on deck, but during the worst times, we got suited up] for watch and put the same dank, damp, wet, chill, sweaty-salty clothes and gear back on, like a recurring nightmare from which there was no hope of awakening. Sometimes there was an emergency and we all had to turn out on deck even if we were off watch and exhausted.

The *Mary Rose's* voyage was a shakedown cruise as well as a delivery, and as every sailor and skipper knows, a shakedown cruise is the time when everything that can go wrong will go wrong, with a few bonus breakdowns or failures thrown in for good measure. One failure we noted a few days into the voyage was that the fresh water maker wasn't working right. This reverse-osmosis machine makes fresh water from seawater at a rate of 5 gallons per hour, which is why, apparently, the *Mary Rose* has only a 60-gallon fresh-water tank. 60 gallons doesn't go very far with four fellows aboard who need to wash themselves, drink, cook, and clean dishes. So, we had to conserve water, but even so, we did not have enough water to reach Tortola. Compounding the problem was the apparent fact that there was water remaining in the tank from, quite possibly, before *Mary Rose's* restoration, a year or two old in a metal tank, and when Captain Tom topped off the tank before our departure, he

32

neglected to flush the tank out before adding fresh water. The result was the worst tank water I had ever tasted – it made me gag one morning, even though I was awfully thirsty. Metallic, stale, and musty, it tasted as though someone had blown down a boiler into the tank, I thought, and was utterly horrible. Since we were far out at sea, Captain Tom decided to stop in Bermuda, where we could repair the water maker, top off the fuel tanks, and get a day's rest in flat water. It had been a rough, cold week and we needed a break anyway. We arrived on Saturday, just as another 40-knot gale was whipping up the seas.

It was a good decision; after clearing customs and refueling/rewatering *Mary Rose*, we had the chance to go ashore, have a few cold beers, and relax for a day. Captain Tom repaired the water maker, and from that point on, we had sweeter and sweeter fresh water, with the memory of that horrible sludge from the first leg of the trip finally diminishing in memory as we neared Tortola. After repairing the water maker, Captain Tom slept for 12 hours straight.

We left the next day, Sunday, in the afternoon. Although I was a little reluctant to leave this pretty place with its turquoise harbor waters behind and head once again out into the unknown of the North Atlantic, I now had more confidence in the *Mary Rose*, in my Captain, and in Jason and Andy; these were capable, brave fellows, and we had, through the crucible of the gale, become a closer team, shipmates and friends, as much as we were remarkably different individuals. Going through rough times at sea together makes a tight crew, even if its members are people with little in common on the land, and who would probably not normally become friends, or close friends, due to disparate personalities and interests. It is a different sort of friendship, developed of necessity, common weal, common risk, and shared exposure to danger and harsh conditions, where the absolute focus of mind, body, and energies is bringing the ship safely to port.

When we left Bermuda, I felt the familiar pang of anxiety, of separation from the land, of a wish, after darkness fell, that the fading glow of the island on the horizon astern would not disappear, but remain with us. The smell of the land had once again vanished, leaving us with the cloying salt tang of the Deep, and my uneasiness would not go away. We were motor-sailing in moderate airs, heading off the wind, and we had engaged the autopilot, whom I judged the best helmsman second to myself, and thoroughly indefatigable, unerringly accurate, and quite capable now that the high seas of the first leg of our passage were, at least for the time being, behind us. So we sat in the cockpit, checking the navigation system, keeping a lookout for other vessels, and occasionally taking turns going below for a hot cup of tea or a snack, usually multi-grain bread smeared with chunky peanut butter. But my uneasiness would not go away, and I was still tired, drowsy, nearly nodding off, when I heard something, a sound that made the hair stand up on the back of my neck (or so I thought) and sent a shiver through me, a shiver of what I can only describe as deep, subliminal terror. I heard music. It was unearthly, ethereal, and faint, like a choir of angels; the music was high, and strange, just out of my range of hearing, and the more I strained to hear it, the more elusive it became. I was fully awake now, and intensely focused, entranced; the music came from nowhere, and everywhere at once, and was incredibly lush and melodic, ornate, sweet, complex, and captivating, yet again, just beyond the range of actual hearing, yet I knew that I was hearing it with my ears. I thought of Mozart, writing for the choirs of angels; no music ever heard on earth; the singing of the sirens. But then came the darker thought; what grave of sunken souls at the bottom of the abyssal plain has the shadow of our keel crossed this night? What sad wreck of drowned souls in the still blackness of the depths has the proximity of our passage disturbed? *Los Cantos de Los Muertos.* I whispered a prayer for them, if indeed we had passed over a wreck. Jay came back on deck with a cup of tea and a sandwich; this broke the spell, and I heard the music no more that night, or any night, but the memory of it haunted me for days afterward.

Now we were experiencing increasingly better, and warmer, weather that continued to improve for the rest of the trip; favorable winds on the beam that pushed the *Mary Rose* through the sea at 9 and even 10 knots at times, for three days in a row, averaging nearly 200 miles per day for about three days. The performance qualities that Captain Nat had designed into her became apparent then, in addition to her strength and seaworthiness. With moderating seas we slept better, ate better, and took turns cooking and preparing the day's main meal in the galley, and regaining our strength. In fact, the winds and seas eventually became quite calm, so much so that we were motoring once again, and would have welcomed a moderate breeze again to move us along, but it remained calm for the final few days of the trip.

By the end of the second week we were in Tortola, arriving on that Saturday, December 4, sitting on the foredeck at break of dawn and seeing the blue outline of the mountainous islands, and our channel between Jost Van Dyke and Tobago islands ahead. We motored into Soper's Hole on the west end of the island around mid-day, cleared customs, and went ashore to explore the harbor and the watering holes.

In the Caribbean, most visiting boats moor, or anchor, and the way one gets to shore, to another boat, or to the bar, is via inflatable, motorized dinghy. Jason and Andy had worked hard the day before to ready the *Mary Rose's* old, sun-baked, rubber inflatable, a thing that looked for all the world as though it had been conceived and built from the sap of the very first rubber tree that grew in Eden. The forward part of it would not hold air for very long, and after Tom, Andy, and Jason had made a valiant attempt at patching its holes, it held air for a little while longer, but still needed occasional re-pressurizing with the foot pump. It looked as though it belonged to one of the natives, or some expatriate down on his luck. On top of that it leaked water, and the hand-pump could not empty it, so the best way to get it dry was to operate it at speed so that its leaky hull would self-bail.

Our favorite watering-hole, almost immediately, was the Jolly Roger, a water-side gathering place for cruisers, expatriates, boat bums, and other similarly distinguished folks on the north side of the harbor. In the open-air Jolly Roger bar at night, one meets everyone who lives out on a moored or anchored yacht, and who has come ashore for the evening, the dinghy dock crowded with inflatables nose-in and nestled together, waiting obediently at the ends of their painters. There is laughter; there are friends new and old to meet or become re-acquainted with; the sun sets in a blaze of color, the dark rounded peaks silhouetted against the fiery sunset as the first bright stars peek out of the deep blue that slowly descents in the west with the last curtain-call of the day. Laughter and eager conversations ring out; the aroma of food grilling on the barbecue grill wafts about, spreading its happy news of steaks and spiny lobster.

It is my last evening in paradise; Captain Tom and I are on a mid-day flight tomorrow to San Juan, Philadelphia, and at last, Providence. I should feel sad, but I do not; too much happiness is welling in my soul. Our voyage was a success; I am with my ship-mates and friends with whom I have been through ordeals as well as swell times, adventure and discovery, and have lived not only to tell about it but to savor this moment. Another round of rum punch comes to the table; we three crewmen of the *Mary Rose* stand and toast our Captain; and suddenly and spontaneously, nearly every-one seated at the tables around us, hearing what we were about and most of them already familiar with our story, rises and joins in, with hearty shouts and earnest well-wishing, much to our delight and surprise. It is the community, the fellowship of cruisers and adven-turers, *Hermandad de La Mar*, the Brotherhood of the Sea. Captain Tom is grinning; this is his moment, saluted by his crew and fellow captains and sailors and bon vivants all encircling. We vow to return again, and to meet again. But for now, we will think only of the joy of this moment; tomorrow is a different day, and by God, it ain't here yet!

◆◆◆◆◆◆◆

Church's Beach

There is a crescent-shaped sandy beach on an island in New England where the salt water is crisply cool and very clear, almost like spring water, where you can watch the sun set in an orange fireball over the sea on a summer evening and where there is almost always some low surf. It is odd, of course, to be on any beach in New England and see the sun set over only water and not a coastline; one would naturally expect a sea-sunset to be characteristic of a California beach on the broad Pacific. Certainly the water on this beach is cold like the Pacific. Yet I have been on this beach at day's end, immersed in the bracingly cold water, even in August, waving my arms to keep my body stationary in the surge, and watched the sun set over Buzzard's Bay, the prevailing southwesterly blowing in my face and the rich salt-sweet chill fresh-lobstery aroma of the deep in my nostrils. The beach faces westward, and there is just enough distance between it and Sakonnet Point to put the land just beyond the horizon. I could pretend that I am somewhere else, but there is no need; this place is wonderful enough.

Up on the beach there is sand, ivory-white, deep and dry forming little dunes and studded with dune grass and beach pea, with occasional clumps of wild beach rose or Rosa Rugosa. My friend Bruce loves this beach; it is his favorite beach in all the world, and he takes no time at all to get wet; whereas I prolong the pain, he runs down the steep beach at a good clip and dives into the surf, then swims out into the swell, sounding and blowing like a porpoise and thoroughly enjoying himself. When you come out of the water, the sheltering warmth of even a threadbare towel feels welcome.

This rare place is known as Church's Beach, on Cuttyhunk Island, a small gravelly pile of terminal moraine at the end of the Elizabeth Island chain, the last bit of land jutting out into Buzzard's Bay. The beach is perhaps no more than a quarter mile long, with only a fraction of that usable, for the southwesterly end of it is all rocky. Sometimes the winter gales take the sand away and one spring Bruce and I went there and saw that the sand was gone; he shook his head sadly. But then we were back, as luck would have it, barely two weeks later and a change in the currents and the magic of nature had somehow returned tons of it to the beach, filling all the spaces between the round cobbles of the bottom and making a smooth, ripply, sandy, soft beach again charged every few seconds with another happy frothy laughing surge running up the incline only to fall back again and fade into the beach itself on its way down.

On a hot summer afternoon the water is deep blue, a clear and beautiful blue, and there is always a breeze from the southwest and the distant land of Westport, off to the north, looks deep blue or purple, undulating along the horizon. It is pleasant to float in the swells of the ocean-clean water and watch the sailboats in the distance beating to windward, heading out of the bay, or running before the wind, slow-motion and billowing white sails, cruising up the bay to the islands, the Cape, or to the Cape Cod canal and who knows what destinations beyond. It is a sweet place and for those moored in Cuttyhunk's quiet inner harbor, one can always hear the surf on Church's Beach on a still night, as regular as a heartbeat, the ever-present scent of the sea and the wild rose and honeysuckle on shore to perfume the air.

◆◆◆◆◆◆◆

Kenny Goes Home

In the morning I was in the ship's big lavatory, washing and bleaching out a pair of white trousers when a fellow seaman named Doyle, walked up to the sink next to me and told me that Kenny had gone missing. I was standing next to one of the round stainless-steel sinks that stood in a long row beneath a mirror-lined wall. I was concentrating on a stain – spaghetti sauce or something of that nature – when Doyle walked up. I didn't really take notice of him standing there – the stain was stubborn – until I noticed that he was not running the water, and when I looked up at him he asked me if I had heard about Kenny.

"No," I replied. Then he said something to me about a bunch of the guys going swimming last night, late, down by the Galveston shore. "We lost Kenny," he said.

"What?"

"He was out quite a ways, it was pretty dark, and then someone noticed that he wasn't there, no one knew where he was." He said this in low tones.

I felt disbelief; I stopped what I was doing. "He must have come in to shore," I offered.

"Nope."

"Well, he has to be all right," I said, not really grasping or believing what Doyle was telling me. Doyle walked away.

Our Coast Guard ship had put into Galveston for a few days. We had been on assignment in the Gulf; the Marine Science Technicians, or MSTs, had been taking water samples, temperature, and other data at various depths for the NOAA weather service, and we had come in for fuel and supplies. We had been at sea for a couple of weeks. It was quite warm – late summer – out on the Gulf and the water was a beautiful deep lovely blue but the weather was generally fine and pleasant and as a result the duty was fairly boring after the first couple of days. The ship moved slowly, the MSTs did their work, and the deck crew did the usual chipping and painting and watch standing. One day some squalls came through as we were heading to the next sampling location and a funnel cloud came down from a dark mass of clouds ahead of the ship. It was beginning to descend, well on its way to becoming a water spout, and the Old Man halted the ship and waited for it to pass. It never touched the water but it was an interesting phenomenon to watch and one of the officers commented that a waterspout, if it hit the ship, could do some damage and no one wanted any of that, so we would wait a few minutes to see what happened. The almost-waterspout was all the excitement we'd had for nearly a month of this oceanographic work out on the Gulf in summer.

So when we heard that we were finally going to take a break and go into Galveston, we were all fairly pleased with the news. It wasn't the choicest place to go, but it was land, it was a port, there would be liberty, and that meant dry land, a change of scenery, bars, and girls. I had never been to Galveston before, so I looked forward to visiting a new place.

It was a long time ago and I do not remember a great deal about Galveston. It was surely much different then than it is today. I remember the long rocky breakwater in the harbor, the steep beaches where they told us that the undertow was pretty severe, big piers along the waterfront, high on pilings, and oil rigs visible out on the horizon. The first afternoon that we had liberty, one of the seamen had a car available and several of us piled in and rode around Galveston and along the barrier islands connected to it. At some point we ended up on a flat beach somewhere that had a shantytown on it, and it looked to be inhabited by Mexicans. We drove through it, people everywhere looking at us, streets of hard-packed sand, but I don't remember where it was. Galveston was a curious, odd place, I thought.

But Kenny and a group of seamen had gone out drinking that Friday night and were drinking hard, and afterward had decided to go swimming, around one in the morning, on the steep beach by the piers that was marked "no swimming" where someone had remarked about the undertow and the strong currents and surf. They were all very drunk and Kenny along with them, and while they were out swimming in the darkness Kenny simply disappeared, slipped under the waves without a sound. One of the guys noticed that they had not heard from him for a few minutes and looked around to the last place that he had been and he was not there anymore.

I first became acquainted with Kenny on the midwatch, standing lookout on the flying bridge of the ship from midnight until four in the morning, while the ship was under way out in the Gulf. The nights were warm and humid and the phosphorescence in the water glowed green and blue around the ship. Only seamen were assigned the job of lookout, and the lookout's job was to keep a sharp eye out for contacts – lights from other ships – and inform the bridge below, even though the exercise was basically useless because the ship's sophisticated radar could pick up everything from the bow to the horizon and at far greater distances than our eyes could usually see in the humid nighttime haze that hung over the sea. The bridge was one story below and the usual personnel on duty at that time would have been the helmsman, a seaman or Boatswain's Mate 3rd class, or BM3, and possibly one of the ensigns, the Officer of the Deck or OOD.

Sometimes the cranky old BM Chief, Chief Smith, was on the bridge during the earlier evening hours and his favorite game was to watch the radar, to see when it picked up a contact at a great distance; he would then look in that direction until he could barely pick up a visible speck of light, since he knew where to look, and then would call down the lookout and dress him down. "My old eyes saw that contact before you did! What's the matter with you, not paying attention? If I see one more contact before you do, you're liberty is canceled this weekend" or such, or he would assign the seaman to some miserable task that no one else wanted to do. Inevitably, he always saw another contact before the lookout did, and made good with his threat. That was his way of getting 'volunteers' for the ship's dirtiest jobs, especially on weekends. To compound matters, by some remarkable quirk of fate, we had an entire ship full of guys like Chief Smith, all of course above the rank of seaman. But I digress.

The flying bridge was actually rather large in area and one had to climb a ladder to get up there. The Chiefs and officers rarely ever went up there, and never at night. They could not be bothered, really, so it became a sanctuary for seamen, especially late at night. There was a wonderful old compass up there mounted on a beautiful sturdy yellow oaken base that was as high as your chest and housed in a heavy brass binnacle. Big iron quadrantial spheres, or Navigator's balls, painted red and green respectively for port and starboard, used to compensate the compass for deviation on an iron ship, were mounted on either side and were as large as cannon balls. A soft golden glow emanated from a lamp inside, illuminating the compass card at night. The compass and binnacle dated from the building of the ship – 1944 – and although nobody used it now because the ship was equipped with an internal gyrocompass,

I used to enjoy gazing at it at night, and besides it was there as a backup in case the gyrocompass failed, which it actually did once or twice.

One fellow strung a hammock up there just for fun, to nap in when he was not on lookout duty; at other times at night, other seamen or firemen on watch with nothing to do, or simply ones who could not sleep, congregated up there to chat, smoke our pipes, and speak in low tones (since the leadership on the bridge did not want us concentrating on anything but avoiding collisions by detecting critical 'contacts'), so that we would not be heard and chastised. Sometimes a fellow would bring up some coffee fro the others; always there was the throaty roar of the engines reverberating through the stack, and the diesel smoke billowing astern from the top of the stack well above our heads. The weather was usually warm, and we could spend hours up there talking about our pasts, our girlfriends back home, the meaning of life, and the entire universe of subjects. There is something about being at sea in the middle of the night under God's great canopy of stars that stimulates such conversation and contemplation in even the dullest fellow. One was rarely alone up there during the middle of the night watches.

Kenny was also a seaman but a few years older than the rest of us. He was thin and slight of build, hollow-cheeked, gaunt-looking, very much the apotheosis of a backwoods Southern boy. He hailed from a tiny place named Greenfield, Miss., way up in the woods, as far from the ocean, just about, as one could get in the deep South and he had a thick drawl, slow manner of speaking, and dry, self-deprecating sense of humor. He was a real country fellow who seemed to like everyone, took everyone at face value and every bump in the road philosophically in stride. He wished no one any harm, not ever, and was well liked aboard by his shipmates, even though he occasionally got in trouble for drinking too much. It was infrequent that he did, usually on liberty on the first night ashore with his mates, and he liked his weed, too – this was the mid-1970s, and practically all the enlisted fellows aboard did, which also got him into occasional trouble.

But by some unhappy instance, a few years earlier, when he had been stationed in Alaska, he beat the tar out of his Executive Officer, or XO, and as a result was busted back to Seaman Apprentice, the lowest rate in the Coast Guard, and a few extra

42

years were tacked on to his enlistment. He had, in fact, been only a few weeks short of getting out of the service; he had done a four-year hitch, and had been looking forward to going home to Greenfield. But there was some problem, the station's XO did not like him, or as the story goes, actually liked him quite a bit in the wrong way and had made an improper sexual advance, and Kenny had rejected it. The XO then brought Kenny up on some trumped-up false charge in retaliation, dereliction of duty or something of similar nature, and Kenny had imbibed some liquor and had caught the XO in town off duty one night and had whaled the bejesus out of him.

When Kenny told me this one evening, I figured that the XO had been a small fellow, or Kenny had been incredibly angry, because the wiry, scrawny Kenny did not look like he could beat a spider into submission, but looks are always deceiving. Kenny was the sort who, slow to anger, might become a fury once aroused. He hated hazing and injustice, lies and meanspiritedness. He was a mellow, laid-back sort of fellow who was easy to be around.

Kenny spent some time in the brig and also had time added to his enlistment. He had never advanced afterward; he was still a sea-man, but over time he had learned how to get along even when pressed and keep his mouth shut, and had kept out of trouble when drinking, even though it was clear that he was at odds with the mil-itary life. Now, he told us, a few weeks hence, when we returned to the ship's home port of Gulfport, his enlistment would be up and he would finally be going home and he had promised himself that he would not look back. He spoke of Greenfield often, his old friends, and how he yearned to get back there. A few weeks after this last stop in Galveston he would be on his way.

Now he was gone anyway and there was nothing that anyone could do about it. Our ship had its orders. I thought it would be appropriate if Kenny was found and his remains brought home to Gulfport aboard his unit, but by the time we had to leave after a few days they still had not found Kenny. I remember the image of the long rock jetties as we steamed out of port onto the broad Gulf, and the same image came back to me a few days later when we heard that Kenny's body had washed up on one of the jetties outside the harbor. So he had gotten off the ship after all, and earlier as well, but in the wrong way and in the end it did not seem fair, not fair at all. But it was just another hard lesson in a quick succession of hard

43

lessons to be learned for me, a very naïve young man of 18 years who, at the time, was going through the experience of watching all of his cherished dreams, ideals, and expectations turned on their heads or falling over like dominoes in the harsh light of day to day reality. And so I lost a friend, not the first, not the last. Life is not fair. Nor is it gentle.

They shipped Kenny's body home to his beloved Greenfield for burial, and of course there was no service for him on the ship and we went back to chipping and painting as before. But one afternoon only a few days later Chief Smith called the seamen in the Deck Force, as we were known, together down to the sail locker and we pulled up chairs on the steel deck surrounded by bins filled with needle guns, hardhats, chipping hammers, and chain gripes and listened to the Chief tell us that the one thing that he liked most about Kenny was that when the going got tough, Kenny wouldn't say anything but just shrug his shoulders and smile and keep on plugging along. Chief was trying to be profound, to use Kenny as an example of how we should handle the low points on a ship whose morale was already lower than the keel and mostly because the ship was top-heavy with a parcel of petty jerks with gold-plated collar devices running it. We all listened politely to the BM Chief knowing that it was pure horseshit because Chief had never really liked Kenny anyhow and had picked on and taunted him, just like he did not particularly like any of us either. But that was how Kenny got out of the Coast Guard and finally found his way home.

◆◆◆◆◆◆◆

Bermuda Dreaming

Sometimes one gets taken by surprise, caught off guard. I went out this morning to town on an insignificant errand. The nuisance storm that had assailed our land's world for the past two days was passing off to somewhere else, taking its gloomy gray skies and rain with it. But when I stepped out into the day, I noticed immediately the low scudding clouds, the freshening wind smelling of the sea, the unseasonable warmth and the sticky humidity, and I realized that this was the same sort of morning as last November, nearly a year ago, when we had sailed into St. George's, Bermuda, after a stormy, cold crossing from Newport and a wild, exhausting night beating back and forth offshore whilst waiting for the light of day so that we could safely make our way into the harbor.

As I sensed this, I was immediately drenched by an equally-unexpected rogue wave of melancholy washing over me, the kind of melancholy that a man may feel when left on the beach, while others sail away; or perhaps even a man bound and harnessed, feet in his traces, with no option but to continue pulling endlessly like an ox for his daily bread while time and life slip away, and opportunities for exploration, adventure, and mental and physical refreshment diminish as the road to life's terminus grows ever shorter. I looked around, frantically, and saw only my life, proscribed by circumstances, with its attendant baggage of stagnation, frustration, and endless demands. I turned, turned again, and found I had made a complete circle, like a broken compass, knowing no direction for progress away from the center.

I yearn to go, but not on a comfortable cruise-ship; I don't want a stateroom, but rather a hammock in the fo'c'sle. Give me strong black coffee and let me handle rough lines in the middle of the night. Let me know the feeling of being there, for then I will know that I am truly alive.

I remember that it was still blowing half a gale on deck as we motored around the channel markers and into the narrow cut – Town Cut – channel blasted through a limestone cliff – and into a strange calm peacefulness that we had not known for a week. It was sunrise, orange, groggy, damp, fatigued sunrise, my mind dulled by lack of sleep, sights and sounds coming to me as through a frosted lens, fuzzy and dark around the edges.

45

Scrubby trees resembling windswept evergreens clung tenaciously to the rocky ledges around the harbor entrance and for the first time I realized that the strange sweet scent reaching my nostrils was the smell of land. Land does have an aroma, indeed, but one is not conscious of it until one has been away from it for a little while.

We passed through the cut and into the snug harbor lined with steep, close hillsides and pastel houses perched on their slopes, with tall palm trees between them. The strong wind made the palm fronds rustle noisily and angrily, and sent low clouds scudding across the sky seemingly barely above the rooftops. The branches and fronds on the top of every spindly-trunked palm tree had been turned into a windsock.

But now, my daydream was over; there was work to do, so once again I put my dreams aside, returned to the present, and drove home.

◆◆◆◆◆◆◆

Sailing Up the Historic Coast to Maine

Sailing to Maine! Anticipation of the trip quickened my pulse, and filled me with childlike eagerness and excitement. Our boat, a J/37 performance cruising sailboat, waited patiently at the dock in Plymouth, Mass., as the orange July sunrise and warm humidity betokened a hot day. But the forecaster's promise of a brisk westerly wind, the result of the passage of a cool front from the north the night before, would hopefully provide relief.

My 20-year old son Tom and I put our bags aboard as my wife Denise saw us off; she had dropped us off at the marina and would drive the car home. The water was still; gulls circled about; a zephyr from the northwest fanned my cheek. The early morning drive had taken us through the winding streets of old Plymouth, clustered clapboard houses with massive central chimneys, chunked together on either side like a monopoly board that had been jostled. Could there be any place in America more storied, more steeped in the earliest history of this country, than Plymouth's waterfront? In my mind, our J/37 became a 17th-Century shallop on a dangerous voyage up the sparsely-populated coast. This trip was simply a boat delivery for a broker, but I asked myself, why allow it to be ho-hum? The mind is its own place, as Milton said, and with the help of my imagination, would turn a chore into an adventure; indeed I was determined that it would.

The sloop's little Volvo diesel grumbled to life; we cast off, and eased her into the fairway and through the mooring field. The wind came up fresh and strong out of the northwest as we followed an eager lobsterman out through Plymouth's winding channel and past the Gurnet. Flat, shallow, inviting Duxbury Bay stretched away inside the shelter of the Gurnet, to the north. I made a mental note to explore it, someday. In addition to my own notebook computer (hastily jump-wired into the radio circuit) with GPS and chart plotter, I also carried with me my dog-eared 1902 copy of Samuel Adams Drake's *New England Legends and Folk Lore*, long a favorite. For I was thinking that this voyage, which in the end would take 18 tiring hours, passes by some of the most historic and legendary territory of the coast of New England, involving the coastlines of three states, and everything from the earliest settlements to battlegrounds to pirate lairs of old, landmarks and treacherous shoals are described and recounted in Drake's wonderful book.

I eagerly anticipated the promised west wind, but it never came. Instead, it blew stiffly, and occasionally unreliably, directly out of the northwest. That made our trip a windward beat the entire way – a single port tack for nearly 100 miles. Sometimes it was wet, as the boat's dodger had not been rigged. But it was exciting work, with whitecaps blowing across Massachusetts Bay for most of the morning, the tiny bluish skyline of Boston visible off the port beam, and in sight for hours on end as we clawed our way toward distant, unseen Cape Ann.

This is a coastline I have traveled many times by Interstate 95, and have sailed out of at various points, but now I was connecting the dots. Blue sea, blue sky; the high land of the South Shore – Ocean Bluff, Scituate – remained visible for hours as we crossed Massachusetts Bay far out, and didn't disappear until we were quite near Gloucester. The strong wind filled our boat's big tawny Kevlar main. We rolled out the 130 Genoa only halfway, and that was plenty, for the lee rail was spending as much time underwater as the keel was. But it was glorious sailing! I thought of how, in the 17th Century, no Boston skyline would have been visible from here. In the distance I spied Boston Light, and the big white wind turbine at Pemberton Point in Hull.

We never went in close enough to follow the curve of the coastline under Cape Ann; to see once-strange Marblehead, where fisherman Philip Ashton became, for some time, a captive pressed member of a pirate crew in 1722; the strange origins of the tale of Skipper Ireson, tarred and feathered and immortalized by Whittier; but soon we were in sight of rocky, forbidding Thacher's island with its twin stone lighthouses. Strong currents swirl around that place, the very outermost part of Cape Ann, and on this day we were stemming a strong current flowing from the north. Thacher's is named for poor Anthony Thacher, who was shipwrecked on the island with his family in August 1635 by a hurricane, and was forced to survive there for some time, eventually escaping back to the mainland, but at the loss of most of his family during the ordeal.

As a sailing friend of mine recently commented that when sailing the coast north, after Gloucester Harbor, "You're going to Maine", meaning, quite accurately, that there is virtually no easy place to tuck into for the night until one reaches Portland. The

Merrimack River has a vicious current; I know that this is so, since I once lived in Newburyport Mass, along its banks. Anchoring is discouraged, and there are few piers or dockage facilities for transients. The same is true, I am told, for Portsmouth, New Hampshire and the Piscataqua River. Well certainly there are a few harbors and rivers, usually shallow, narrow, lined with sandbars and shoals (such as the Hampton River), and York Harbor, Maine, seems pleasant but small, and you had better know your way in and around.

We sailed past the distant, bluish, undulating hills of the North Shore, Ipswich, Newbury, and farther, and I remember how lovely the ancient land looked from the sea. Since major topography doesn't change much in 300 years, I imagined that my view was not much different from what the captain of my imaginary shallop might have seen on his way up the coast. Here, he would know that there were settlements ashore, if he had need to take his vessel to land; but the further north he went, to Maine, the more likely the shore dwellers would be native peoples, and not necessarily friendly to stranded Englishmen.

Catching a glimpse of a familiar landmark is always a comfort. It lets one know, with some accuracy, one's approximate location, and that you are making progress toward your destination. Otherwise all you have to go by is your chart and the boat's apparent wake.

It took forever, like losing the Boston skyline, to put Thacher's over the horizon. We sailed past the starkly beautiful Isles of Shoals – no protection or anchorage there – a rumored hiding place for pirate treasure, a place where a number of silver bars were discovered in the 19th Century by a land-owner who reportedly used the proceeds to construct a needed breakwater.

I saw the unmistakable arched I-95 highway bridge over the Piscataqua, the high bridge that connects Portsmouth, New Hampshire to Kittery, Maine, and this cheered me. Mount Agamenticus loomed ahead, surrounded by piney green; full-sized sailboats with sails seemingly the size of tiny white butterfly wings skimmed and passed to and fro across the surface, in slow motion, miles distant. We would see Agamenticus for hours yet, only losing sight of it near dusk as we approached Kennebunkport. In Adams' book, Agamenticus is a great landmark, the Sailor's Mountain, visible for sixty miles in either direction up and down the coast. The

Native peoples considered it a sacred place, he relates, and folklorists have woven the "Indian legend of Saint Aspenquid, whom some writers have identified with the patriarch Passaconaway" around it. Passaconaway was the great Sachem who lived to a very advanced age, and who sadly foretold the demise of the Native peoples in the face of European expansion in New England.

We sailed onward past Point Neddick, past The Nubble as the sun was sinking low in the sky; looked out at distant, lonely Boon Island, where ten of the poor shipwrecked sailors of the merchant ship Nottingham Galley were stranded for twenty-four days in the wintry months of 1710, resorting to cannibalism before they were finally rescued. Along this coast, I was amazed at the tens of thousands of lobster buoys everywhere – perhaps more pots and buoys than lobsters – stretching on for miles and endless miles. The sunset was flaming, wildly beautiful; and to the east, a three-quarters moon rose out of a pinkish luminous haze above the horizon. The wind died at dusk, off Cape Porpoise; thereafter we motored over calm seas under a brightening orb.

The most brilliantly lit part of the entire coast was Old Orchard Beach. We watched fireworks burst in the distant sky above the town, and it seemed, miles away, to be an island of celebration and frivolity amidst the deepening darkness of the coast.

In time, we rounded Cape Elizabeth, and began heading up toward Hussey Sound; our goal was a marina in Falmouth. The cool, clammy-sweet scent of the deep left us, replaced by the complex, warmer scent of the land, borne on the gentle night-currents of air still floating down from the west. Islands now surrounded us everywhere, and blinking lights of all colors mounted on channel markers, ledges and shoals made it a potentially confusing situation, but I had done my homework. Strange birds made odd calls and sounds in the trees on the many wooded islets and peninsulas that we passed. I caught the scent of flowers, and honeysuckle, mingled with the incense-like aroma of wood fires, from cottage fireplaces and camps.

Finally, at 1:30 in the morning, we gently edged up to the dock, secured our vessel, and in the cool stillness of the Maine night, turned in for a well-earned, bone-weary rest and sleep.

In the bright morning, I looked around at the beautiful scenery, and was told that these were the 'Calendar Islands', so named because there is an island for every day in the calendar; and I secretly promised myself that I must, unquestionably, return soon in my own boat and explore this wonderful Maine coast which, I suddenly realized, I could never live long enough to grow weary of exploring.

◆◆◆◆◆◆◆

Voices among the Cellar Holes

It all began at the Whaling Museum in New Bedford – but oddly enough, it was less about whaling than about something else – typical for me.

When I was a young boy – before my teenage years – my grandfather often took my cousin and I to visit the Whaling Museum in New Bedford occasionally on a gray wintry Saturday when there was not much else to do and the weather was not conducive to outdoor activity. It is not a long trip to New Bedford from where we lived in the East Bay area of Rhode Island – maybe a half-hour at best – but it seemed much longer then. We boys rode in Grandpa's old Studebaker and took turns packing his corncob pipe with fresh tobacco. Grandpa had been a boatbuilder before his retirement, among other things, and he was full of the lore of the sea and never missed an opportunity to share it, and the history that he knew, with his young charges. I loved these trips to the museum, because it was, and still is, a very special place, full of bones, blocks, baleen, and musty old marvels too numerous and remarkable to list here.

The Whaling Museum was, and still is, owned and operated by the Old Dartmouth Historical Society, which, in addition to the magnificent centerpiece that is the museum, also had an interest in preserving the history of that delightful little corner of southeastern Massachusetts that includes New Bedford, Westport, and some of the surrounding area, and thus the museum had, in some small part, exhibits relating thereto. But whaling and everything to do with whaling has always been 99 percent of the museum's offering. There seemed to be little else having to do with the rest of Old Dartmouth and its environs, which puzzled me.

Yet oddly enough, my favorite exhibit at the museum, one that was very easy to overlook, had nothing to do with whaling per se. It was a small room that re-created a 17th Century primitive household in what would presumably have been Old Dartmouth in the time of the earliest settlers. It was off in the eastern part of the museum building, a doorway off a hallway, not labeled if I recall, easy to miss, and might have been taken for a broom-closet except that it was not at the end of a hall, and the door was open. It was, in appearance, a dark room, small, lined with brown, rough-hewn beams and bare wooden walls, wide-plank floors and sparse furnishings. There was a big faux field-stone fireplace at one end of it, with a make-believe fire roaring in the hearth, little red coals and gold flames cleverly recreated with lights and technique such that it looked so real that I could swear that I felt the warmth from that primitive hearth when I stood in the room.

Of course, you could not actually go into the exhibit room and touch anything; a small square area inside the doorway was roped off, only enough room to stand and observe. I wanted to go over to the hearth and lie down next to the fire; it seemed like such a cozy, other-worldly place, a window into the past, a place to rest in snug comfort while, I imagined, the sharply-biting cold and sleet of the New-England winter lashed the outside of the crude dwelling and massive mortared gray stone chimney, and the forest primeval, populated by bears and hostile, skulking Indians, encircled it. Indeed, there was a little recording, I think, of wind – howling wind, as one would hear through the chimney-flue – playing over and over again in the background, adding to the ambience of the little place. Although I was young, I clearly understood the message behind it; it was a statement about the tough life that our forebears faced in the primitive land that was 17th Century New England. It spoke of their privations, hardscrabble life, and precarious existence, but also showed that there was yet comfort to be found in home and hearth.

The exhibit remained for many years – I have no idea how long, twenty, maybe thirty years; and as I grew older, and visited the museum less frequently, I nevertheless always made it a point to stick my head into that little doorway, and I had to smile. There was something unchanging and comfortable about it; the same vision, the same room, nothing unmoved; and why not? History is written; it recedes into the past, but it does not change. Facts, as John Adams pointed out, are immutable. The message too is unchanging. In a world where nothing seems sacred anymore, nothing seems stable or noble, everything is in flux, where uncertainty reigns and old values have been turned on their heads, this little room, in later years, offered me a connection to my youth, to the values that a young bright-eyed boy learned and embraced and had reverence for, once upon a time. I hoped that it would always be there.

Time passes all too quickly. The first streaks of gray in the once-boy's hair have spread like mushrooms on a log to a pepper-and-salt beard with more salt than pepper. I went back to the museum a few years ago and to my dismay found the old room walled off, with a note saying that the exhibit area was being remodeled, and soon would offer a new display of some sort. My heart sank; if the 'interpretations' in the rest of the museum are any indicator of direction (and this is true of so many museums nowadays), the new display will be, or is, not about Old Dartmouth, not even about whales, but is quite probably configured as another tiresome paean to "celebrating ethnic diversity" or such, as if we don't have enough of that theme being force-fed to us everywhere we turn nowadays. Is there some point in time when we can collectively get a point across to the politically correct zealots that we do get the message? That we're OK with it? That perhaps it's time to move on and recover a broader and more inclusive view of history, one that once again includes our early local forebears? Perhaps not; the early settlers have too many things going against them, demerit check offs in the enlightened postmodern culture classroom. They were white Europeans; a good many of them males, at that; they were religious; and they even (and unfortunately) shot at Indians occasionally. They often did not pay their help – or themselves – a living wage, and did not practice fair trade. Still, that's enough right there in modern revisionist culture to deny them any creditable place in history, even the place that they heretofore occupied as the founders of the country that we live in at present.

These days I hike the woodland trails of a large preserve in Tiverton, R.I., fairly adjacent to the Massachusetts border and that whole area of Southeastern Massachusetts that contains Westport and Dartmouth. I hike during the cold months of the year, when there are few people to meet on the trails. I hike nearly every day that time permits, sometimes when a lovely dusting of snow has decorated the quiet landscape and my boots crunch with every step. Sometimes I go when the wind is blustering and roars in the bare upper tree branches, and other times yet when the weak winter sun shines golden in the late afternoon on the bright tan beech-leaf carpet of the forest floor and the green Boston ferns that hang from the rocky ledges and will not wilt and curl until they feel the deepest bite of January's freeze.

I hike several miles of trails that include the old Eight Rod Way, an uncompleted road from the 17th Century that had once been planned to run to Plymouth. It is still, in places, paved with the small round cobbles that local farmers painstakingly gathered from their fields to deposit by the wagonload yard by yard over decades. Areas of exposed ledge are worn and rutted from wagon wheels. This area was settled back in the early days by subsistence farmers and pioneers. It is a haunted place and their voices whisper from the old cellar-holes that dot the landscape, foundations often hidden behind groves of lovely green mountain laurel, a shrub that remains green year 'round, even when its upper branches are laden with snow and ice.

Little babbling Borden Brook, dark as English tea from the tannins leaching out of the Ice Age-era remnant cedar swamp from whence it originates in underground springs, murmurs its way through the woods. It flows under heavy stone slab bridges put in place by rough hands three centuries ago. The brook tumbles on happily beneath the jumbled collapsed stones of the raceway of the old Borden sawmill, its foundation and corbelled arch stone bridge still sound since the mill sawed trees into planks for Tiverton village houses in the 18th Century. There may be burials out here; perhaps, deep beneath the soft blanket of oak leaves, tangled brown roots and humus are the bones of Indians who never saw a European face; perhaps there are graves of slaves, or of the very poor, or of the early settlers' children, for their mortality was very high.

I pause at the cellar hole of one man's home, and this one has a name, in the guidebooks – Scipio Cook. I do not know who Scipio Cook, with his classical Roman first name, was, although there must be someplace where I can learn more about him. A little family of chipmunks darts in and out around the mortarless stones of his old foundation, all traces of wood or timber long gone. But I found Scipio's little dug well one day, and the remains of his small garden – for herbs and vegetables, probably turnips and onions for his stew-pot – can still be outlined, for the vegetation is different there.

Farther up the trail, there lies a group of stone-lined cellar holes that is most intriguing, for this was a small, closely situated community or farm with intersecting stone walls. The cellar walls are bulged in, looking as though they are ready to collapse, although they have looked that way, most probably, for more than a century.

But these cellar holes, dating from the First Period, perhaps, are the same size as would fit the little re-created room that used to be in the museum. These were small houses, very small, very simple. Many has been the cold day's hike that I wished, with the rustle of sleet in the upper tree-branches and little crystals speckling my hat and shoulders, that I could walk inside, warm myself by the fire, and have a bowl of stew, perhaps, or tea, at least haven and shelter, brief respite, from the weather, sharing a few moments with these early, hardy people.

There is a new neighborhood development nearby, cutting deeply into the Tiverton woods. Although this preserved place will, by deed, always be protected from the incursion of that development, in the nakedness of winter that plat of vinyl-sided plastic box-houses can occasionally be glimpsed through the woods, their treeless lots and loam-less lawns re-seeded desperately trying to grow grass before the rains gully them. But some of the boxes have fireplaces, though not built with stone or brick chimneys but siding-covered ones with tin caps. Burning seasoned hardwood produces the same aromatic incense no matter what it is burned in, however, and occasionally, as I pass these foundations on a day when the gray sky is lowering and threatening snow, I will catch a whiff of that burning wood, and it will overwhelm my senses. Even though that anonymous early home is no longer here, I can smell the aroma of its hearth on the cold air.

At such times, I will pause at the edge of a cellar hole, whose nameless inhabitants long ago passed to dust, and will whisper a brief prayer for them, to let them know that in the stillness of the woods, decades and even centuries after their hard lives have ended, in a small piece of land that in many ways has begun to resemble once more the world that they lived in, someone remembers them, cherishes the memory of who they were and how they lived, and what they sought to do in carving a settlement out of a howling and unforgiving wilderness. Despite their sufferings and losses, Puritan father William Bradford observed and wrote, "They knew they were pilgrims, and looked not much on those things, but lifted up their eyes to the heavens, their dearest country, and quieted their spirits."

They are remembered now by someone not confused or distracted by the myopic fad-currents of the moment, who does not judge them by today's political cause-driven standards. History, after all, cannot be changed or erased, though many have tried to do both for selfish ends and private agendas. The glass that looks backward can at times be obscured deliberately, ignored, or trivialized; but I stand at the stone doorstep of a yawning hole filled with stumps and leaves, and listen for the whispering voices of the family that once lived there and the wind howling in the flue. It is there, they were there, and always will be for the patient listener with an open and uncluttered mind. Listen not with the ears, but with the heart, and you too will hear them, calling out to be remembered.

◆◆◆◆◆◆◆

First Light of Sombrero Island

I first saw the flash of the Sombrero Island Light while on helm watch in the big catamaran *Cressida*. In the wee hours of the morning, I didn't actually see the light at first, only the reflection of the flash against the murky sky, since the lighthouse was still over the horizon. Yet, the sight of it cheered me; it was the first man-made thing I had seen since a wallowing Russian freighter had passed us like a rust-streaked gray ghost, three miles to windward, five days earlier on a gray, stormy day.

We had been to sea for nearly 10 days now, in contrary winds and occasional bad weather and out of sight of land for almost as long. At night, when it was clear, we searched the sky in vain for the moving lights of airliners high in the stratosphere, but all that we saw were the occasional trails of shooting stars. We were hundreds of miles from land and I had hoped for the welcome signs of other humans in the world – even if distantly aloft. Nor did we see any other vessels of any kind save, at last, for the freighter; for all we knew, we might just as well have been alone on the sea and the only humans in the world. We tried to contact the freighter by radio, but it never answered us.

Now, Sombrero Light was coming up, just beyond the horizon, and I felt an inner joy, peace, and satisfaction. The night was humid and warm, the air dense and misty, and it was almost three o'clock in the morning when I first thought I saw a faint pulse of light on the horizon ahead. I though at first that my eyes were playing tricks on me because I was weary and had not slept well the night before; but no, there it was again – a misty, ghostly pulse at regular intervals – so I knew that it was a navigational beacon. The humid air reflected the flash, carrying its glow over the horizon to me. The chart told me that Sombrero Island was a hat-shaped pile of lifeless rubble still ten miles away or more; it actually looks like a sombrero viewed from the side; but after a thousand miles of ocean, it seemed close enough to reach out and touch.

I was glad for it; I was sick of the boat and sick of being at sea with a nasty jerk for a skipper and both my friend Steve, the hired yacht delivery guy who had invited me along to crew, and I, were desperate to jump off the boat at the first landfall.

During the next hour or more, as we sailed closer and into the Anegada Passage, it grew brighter and brighter until I could actually see the flash. We would pass it in the night, and never see the island or the tower; just as well, I thought, I don't need the temptation, even though, according to the chart, it was a desert; small, rocky, with no water, no habitation or settlement, nothing but an automated beacon surrounded by broken limestone rocks and guano. I would have to restrain my urge – and resolution, made some time earlier - to go ashore at the first spit of land encountered, no matter how inhospitable it might be. Patience, now; just a little longer, I told myself, and I would be on solid ground once more and free of this vessel.

Cressida was nearly out of fresh water, and what was left in the tanks was cloudy and tasted odd, a little bit stale, metallic, something like a pond on a humid day. But it would last, and we would get into St. Martin in all likelihood the following afternoon or evening, if the wind held, and it should, I thought. We were in the trades now, so that in fact we were sailing pretty much around the clock. We would not need the engines much; that was good, because the fuel filters were constantly becoming clogged with contamination, bacterial growth that was occurring in the fuel tanks because skipper Walter hadn't known well enough to put biocide in them. The first hint of trouble had been an unannounced change of engine speed. First it would slow down, and run indecisively, sometimes faster, sometimes slower, then finally slow down and quit.

"Sounds like she's not getting any fuel," Steve had said. "Engine's being starved."

We finally discovered the problem when we pulled the fuel filter; some sort of fuel bug, a fuel-eating microbe, was growing in the diesel tank, clogging the filter, restricting the flow of fuel to the engine and shutting it down. To make matters worse, we had run out of fuel filters. There were two in the little diesel engines in each hull, and two spares. So, we kept swapping the two that we had, using one set while I washed the other out in a sink full of water and detergent. The paper filters came out collapsed and clogged with a brown scum that had to be scrubbed off, rinsed, and blown out from the inside, then dried with a paper towel. The paper vanes of the filters were beginning to look hairy and I was afraid that they were going to disintegrate. We had no more fuel biocide left although at this point it would hardly matter anyhow since the fuel tank was already infected with these little algae or weird micro-organisms or whatever they were that seemed to like the taste of diesel.

Even though Sombrero was uninhabited and distant, the simple fact of its visibility made me feel as though we were at the end of our voyage. The dock could have been 10 feet away; I dearly wished that it were morning, such was my anxiety for the trip to be over. At this point, no problem was insurmountable; everything could be suffered; this was the home stretch.

The steady flashing light was comforting; it reminded me of a time, years earlier, when I was a student in college in southern Rhode Island and I rented a summer cottage for the off-season with a couple of other guys down on Great Island near Point Judith. I was lucky; my bedroom window faced the distant lighthouse, a couple of miles away, and at night I could see its flash from my pillow when I faced the window. I often fell asleep with the distant flash of Point Judith light on my face.

Steve emerged from the darkness of the cabin, startling me slightly. It was his watch time, his turn at the helm. Normally I would go below at that time to wake him, but he was already up, dressed, and ready for his helm trick.

"I was just about to wake you," I said.

"No problem. Couldn't sleep."

"Landfall fever?"

"Yep. Any contacts?"

"Sombrero Light in view," I said. "We're into the Anegada Passage."

"Oh, that's great."

"It's almost over."

"Can't happen soon enough."

"Asshole asleep?"

"Yes, thank God. Okay, what's your heading?"

I briefed him on everything including the trim of the sails, and he took over.

"Have a good rest," Steve said.

"I'm going to have a Scotch and celebrate first," I said. He laughed. "I'll have mine tomorrow in Philipsburg. Or just save some for me."

"I will. There's plenty." And with that I left him and turned in, anxious for the light of morning, and my first glimpse, in a very

60

long time, of the green mountainous land of the island of St. Martin. I could see it in my mind's eye. Anguilla was nearby, in the night; I could almost feel it, taking one last look at the chart and pouring my glass full of the strong amber spirits. I would try to sleep; dawn would be in only a few hours, and I wanted to greet the day refreshed.

◆◆◆◆◆◆◆

Coffee with a 'Stick' in it

Privateer runs on different things; sometimes diesel; sometimes wind; and since she is a gaff bloody hog to windward, sometimes both. The crew, however, runs on coffee, and the crew runs the boat. Without coffee, many a cruise on *Privateer* would not have left the dock on schedule, early in the morning with a fair tide.

The affinity of sailormen for coffee is nothing new. I once read how the old schoonermen in the 19th century practically lived on the stuff as they fished the cold waters of the Atlantic off New England. In those days, the work was hard, the days were long, wet, and cold, and the old wooden schooners were unheated and damp. The men were constantly eating – biscuits, pies, anything with calories in it, and the cook was busy all day and part of the night keeping the cupboards full, and the men drank strong black coffee kept perpetually hot in big enameled steel coffee pots. The expression was that they liked their coffee "Blacker than Sin, and Stronger than Love." We've made it that way, inadvertently, aboard *Privateer* once, after the glass coffeepot had taken a tumble in a spate of rough water and had smashed on the galley deck, and we had to make 'cowboy coffee' by boiling it in a pan and the Master Blender put a little too much coffee into the pan.

It has been, for the longest time, a petty annoyance to me that some folks, including my elder sailing pal Bryce, think a dirty coffee pot makes for more flavorful coffee. I also found this falsehood in the aforementioned book, so the myth goes back to the 19th century, at least, but then again, so does Bryce, methinks sometimes. But a dirty coffee pot does not mean tastier coffee. It means dirty coffee, says I; thus the coffee pot on *Privateer* is washed, at the very least, once a day when at sea.

It takes the aroma of coffee brewing to draw men out of their bunks on a cool summer morning when the departure time is early – sunrise – and the crew was up late the night before keeping the dock awake with the Yo-Ho-Ho-Me-Hearties and such, making frequent trips to the dark end of the floating pier and vowing to plunder the seven seas – all of them – on the morrow. Sleeping on a boat in New England waters is quite different from sleeping at home in your bed; the night grows cool, the blanket warm, comfortable, and cocoon-like; then way too early, the annoying sun peeps down through the portholes, rising at the same time as it does every day but more noticeably on the boat. There is the salt tang of fresh air and the tippity-tap sound of a most damnable sea-bird hopping around the deck above the cabin, looking for a place to dump his dreck before flying off. I reach up with a broom handle to tap the overhead; too late. He's gone, and has left me with the necessity of a morning freshwater hose-down before departure. But no one wants to get out of the rack. It takes the smell of coffee to draw them forth, blinking against the brightness of the sun reflecting back off the oily-smooth harbor waters, rubbing their eyes, stubbing into things as they try to make their way around the cabin. It is full daylight now, but you'd think it was still the middle of the night, or the crew had lost their eyesight.

We debate; does someone drive the mile into town to the doughnut-shop and bring back a group of tall ones, or do we make a pot here, aboard? Remember, the idea of having the crew sleep aboard the night before a weekend trip was not solely to allow the men to drink and swear well out of earshot of their wives far into the night, but also to facilitate an early departure. It's the only way to make it work; otherwise the crew will trickle down to the dock throughout the morning, unprepared (forgot this, forgot that) and you won't get off the dock until shortly before noon, by which time the prevailing onshore wind will have kicked up and it will be a tough, short-tacking annoying slog down Narragansett Bay to get to the open water that we seek.

The early-morning coffee debate, in garbled voices that sound a bit like sideband picked up on a shortwave set, only serve to aggravate the senior member of our crew, Bryce, who is just crawling stiffly out of his bunk. He is, I believe, the singular fellow for whom the term 'curmudgeon' was coined. He begins impatiently banging things about in the galley; gruffly, clumsily. He draws water, lights the galley, he's putting ground coffee into the percolator cup, spilling it everywhere, saying nothing. It is when the normally glib Bryce says nothing that he is best left alone, in much the same way that one would leave an agitated bull in a field alone. Bryce is using our dented aluminum percolator, Old Reliable, that replaced the glass coffee pot after the pot, on its first voyage out past the arm of the Cape, had a rather abrupt encounter with the galley deck because someone had left it on the stove and forgotten to nestle it down in the deep well of the sink with the liquor.

63

Old Reliable makes a great pot of coffee once one learns the true art of percolating. It is a patient art. We have been spoiled at home with drip-coffee makers that are fast but, unfortunately, require 110 volts to operate, not available aboard *Privateer* when she's not dockside, and although her inverter would probably handle the load, I simply don't want to do things that way. Bryce, after all, grew up with percolated coffee; he has taught us the peculiar art of making it. I will add that Bryce truly loves his coffee, more so than anyone I have ever met. He will have two cups to anyone else's one, and be all the livelier for it, as in 'insufferable popinjay', for the balance of the day.

There is a favorite old-time fiddle tune named "Whisky before Breakfast". Bryce must know it. Bryce is a font of sea-lore and tradition, probably due to his maturity and great length of experience on the sea. Many folks believe that wisdom comes with maturity and experience, as a natural and inevitable accompaniment; but Bryce is a living example that this maxim is not necessarily true, but that is a different discussion. One morning, as we were heading south from the harbor, just after sunrise, I was below pouring the coffee; my best sailing buddy Jim was at the helm, and to my great surprise, Bryce handed his full cup of steaming black coffee back to me through the main hatch, only moments after I had passed it to him, with the sour admonition, "Put a stick in it, will you?"

"A what?"

He pointed to the big jug of Gosling's Black Seal rum sitting in the well of the galley sink.

"Aye, sir!" I replied, now grasping his intent. I took the cup, poured a little of the coffee into the sink, and then added a generous dollop of the dark rum – pouring well out of sight of the hatchway, so that Bryce could not see the extent to which I was spiking it – and noted, with amusement, how the color of the beverage did not change at all, though its specific gravity did so, and markedly. I handed it back up. "Just a smidgeon" I said, and waited for the gasp of surprise, and the inevitable epithet – but heard nothing. And so it went.

That's where I learned the meaning of 'put a stick in it', certainly a comment arguably quite male in metaphor, but it became a tradition aboard *Privateer* for some members of the jolly crew to start the day with a 'stick' in their coffee. That very same morning, the tradition became instantly popular, and I must add, even institutionalized; another interpretation of 'The Custom of the Sea." And no, it was not for the Captain, unless the boat was riding at anchor and the balance of the day was to be spent in a dissipated manner. And while it did, undoubtedly, blunt some of the pain of the previous night's overindulgence at the equivalent of the 'Spouter Inn', it was a tradition not to be abused, or trifled with. After a few more 'sticks' in Bryce's coffee, despite the stimulating effects of the brewed bean, by the time we passed under the Newport bridge – a little more than an hour later – Bryce was nowhere to be found in the cockpit, indeed, he was back in his bunk, snoring away and oblivious to the mad dash of Apollo's chariot across the sky.

My favorite experience, come down all the years, is waking up on a cool, bright summer morning in Block Island's New Harbor, way out at the far north end, swinging on an anchor. Old Sol is up and about his business long before anyone else save the bakeryman ashore, despite any promises made, by captain or crew the previous evening, to be up at the crack of dawn. Alarm clocks are not allowed aboard *Privateer*; indeed the last one that made its way aboard, legend has it, found itself on its way to a permanent berth five fathoms below the harbor surface when it was barely into its first solo performance aboard. As many an aspiring diva has learned, audiences can be cruel.

Rather, awaken ye slowly; and before your eyes have yet opened, feel the cool morning puffs of breeze on your face as they waft down the open hatchway to bathe and refresh the cabin. Smell the tang of salt, and the sweet perfume of distant wild roses and honeysuckle on the land, unseen but green and alive in your imagination, a mental picture of a harbor well known and loved, as real in your mind's eye as ever it can be. No slack halyard rattles against the mast; there is only the muted laugh of ripples lapping against the hull. The spot-light of the sun, through a port-light, dances back and forth around the cabin as the boat swings on its mooring, smoothly passing about like globes on an antique planetarium, music of the spheres, crossing your face every once in a while with a momentary patch of bright, orange warmth upon your eyelids; a sea-bird calls. It is time to awaken.

Then I have sat in the cockpit gazing around the harbor, breezy and sparkling in the bright white morning sun, in the cool shade of the Bimini, tiny sparkles of sunlight peeping through the weathered canvas, the deck still damp with dew, nursing a steaming aromatic cup of fresh coffee while Bryce points out and comments on the many diverse craft in the harbor. Doing thus is a favorite morning pastime of his, while the rest of the jolly crew slowly emerge from their bunks and endeavor to rub the goo out of their eyes so that they can properly see the harbor and greet the day. But perhaps the most welcome sight and sound in Block Island's New Harbor, on a sunny morning, brisk, bright, or fogged-in and foul, is Aldo's bakery boat. Aldo – I assume that's his name – rides around the harbor in a Boston Whaler-type open boat every morning, with a young helper usually, his broad-beamed skiff loaded with nice pastries, breakfast sandwiches, and coffee, all on display, the coffee in big square urns. Signal to him or call him on the radio. He's a big fellow – heavyset, camped under a broad-brimmed straw hat, and he will come over and sell coffee and breakfast to you. You can hear him from a good ways off, his deep, strong voice calling out across the water, "Andiamo", the call-word or slogan of Aldo's bakery. I looked up the translation and it apparently means, "We go." I'm not sure how that relates to the bakery boat, other than that they bring it to you; indeed it reminds me more of an aria from Mozart's Marriage of Figaro. Additionally, because Aldo drags out the syllables, I thought, for many years, that he was actually bellowing out "Coffee Aboard, aboard" with a strange accent. But no, I read of late, after being quite wrong all these years, that it's "An-di-a-mooo, a-mooo" as best as I can describe phonetically, sounding a lot like a yodel, of sorts. It doesn't matter anyway, because he does a brisk business; he is the Angel of Coffee to a harbor full of sailors too hung over to make their own pot of java, and as such has helped many a poor miserable soul feel better.

◆◆◆◆◆◆◆

Bryce and the Art of the Deal

My phone rang; it was a call from my older mentor and occasional sailing buddy Bryce, over on the Vineyard. "Moulie, Dickly just called me. There's a big, beautiful Gulfstar 45 for sale in the Globe classified. Asking $69,000. We have to go see it. Here's your next boat!"

I don't know when – or why – Bryce nicknamed me 'Moule', the French term for a 'mussel' – but somehow he latched onto it and it stuck; perhaps we had steamed a pot of them in beer one time or another. But Bryce is a thoroughly interesting fellow, a man of great mind, just so long as one remembers the old adage that the thinnest of boundaries separate genius from madness. He is not from Martha's Vineyard, he only lives there with his wife Delores in a humble dwelling off a dead-end gravel street. He's actually from somewhere around Bridgewater Mass., not even Cape Cod proper, but rather that inner swampy no-man's-land adjacent, where the northern counterpart to the Jersey Devil has been reported in times past. But as Bryce, who is an able self-promoter, has always understood, it's not really about whether you are actually from the Vineyard, it's about making people think that you are, and the consequence of being able to trade on that perception, something that Bryce is always happy to do, being a natural toastmaster and engaging hail-fellow-well-met who is always receptive to a complimentary drink or a dinner invitation.

I had sold my wooden gaff yawl *Privateer* the previous fall and was in the market for a newer, larger boat, this time a fiberglass boat. All my previous boats had been wooden, so the idea of acquiring a 'glass boat was interesting, although a bit daunting, for me, being unexplored territory. I was mildly unsure of myself; but I knew that Bryce would help me. Bryce has always been a big fan of Gulfstar sailboats, I never really learned why, and he loves to sail on them whenever the opportunity presents itself. Everyone knows that buying a boat – particularly a large one – is about more than simply plunking down a fistful of money. It's a bit more involved, something of a little dance, playing a hand of poker, in essence a negotiated deal.

Bryce does not own a boat himself; indeed he has not owned a proper one in all the years that I have known him. His only 'boat' was a discarded beat-up canoe that he and his wife Delores found cast up on a wooded beach in the lagoon down behind their house. Delores insisted that Bryce bring it home and paint it bright orange, so that it could appropriately be named 'Punkin'. She had always wanted a boat named 'Punkin'. This may be why Bryce was always happy to sail on other people's boats, and did quite frequently, often having the use of them for weekends at a time. He is an able sailor who once crewed for Don Street in the Caribbean, and is justly proud of having done so. Indeed, he was the one who had talked me into buying *Privateer* some years earlier, and after I had restored and launched her, began the frequent habit of hopping the Friday afternoon ferry over to New Bedford, so that I could pick him up and take him sailing on *Privateer* for the weekend. It didn't matter that I might have made other plans; whatever they were, after all, they could not be more important than a bellying sail full of wind for two 'men of the sea' as he often said. So there I would find him at the ferry dock, wearing his characteristic Nantucket-red shorts, yellow sou-wester (even in sunshine), and carrying a big duffel bag full of clothes, toiletries, and bottles of warm beer to drink on the ride back from New Bedford to Bristol for a weekend of sailing on Narragansett Bay and beyond.

Oddly enough, the heads-up about the Gulfstar advertisement came from his crotchety, curmudgeonly friend Dick Leigh. Leigh was a funny fellow; he once gave Bryce a scale for a Christmas present, so that Bryce could weigh himself daily to see how much he was overweight. In fact, Bryce isn't and wasn't overweight – rather, Dick Leigh was as skinny as Ichabod Crane, and probably for the same reasons as Ichabod – but he liked rubbing Bryce's nose in their respective physical differences. I thought that his gift of a scale was akin to using deodorant sticks as stocking-stuffers. Finding the old crank insufferable (indeed he once sneeringly referred to Delores, who is actually a native of the Vineyard, as 'that dame from the Cape'), I shortened his name to a single word, 'Dickly', so that it could be used as an adjective. It stuck, at least with Bryce and me.

But it had been a raw, wet, gray, sleety April and now it was nearly mid-May and signs of spring were nowhere in evidence, and here was some poor sot in Onset selling his 1986 Gulfstar Hirsch 45-foot sailboat through of all things a cheap classified ad in the Globe newspaper. No broker listing. I phoned him, his name was

Tony, and I made an appointment to see the boat at its slip in a couple of days down in Onset. When asked, he replied that there had not been much other interest in it – thus far.

The day was rainy and cold when Bryce and I walked down to the dock at the marina. The boat was big, white, modern (compared to what I was used to) and very nice looking. But we saw, as we approached, that something was wrong – the roller-furled jib was roller furled the opposite way, i.e., inside out – with part of the sun cover inner seam showing so that it looked slightly like a barber-shop-pole of alternating blue and white stripes, or something out of a Venetian carnival.

The gate on the dock was locked – the combination that Tony had given me didn't work – so I had to call him, cell phone to cell phone. He came out of the cockpit and bounded up the dock, a short, rotund, energetic Mediterranean sort of fellow in a tank-top tee-shirt, fast-talking, sporting a profusion of gaudy jewelry, two days' growth of beard, and seeming to be a little bit flustered for some reason. "This is my friend Bryce" I said, by way of introduction. "Sailing buddy, came along for the ride." Tony gave Bryce a wary look, then turned and led us down the finger pier to the boat.

It was immediately clear, belowdecks, that the boat was a mess. One berth in the main saloon had been badly modified to make it into a 'love couch' of sorts with a rickety round table on a pedestal screwed to the deck. Little votive and scented candles were lit everywhere. The boat smelled of sour water, mildew, and dampness. I could see that the port-lights had not been closed properly; there was water seepage throughout. There was no dinette table in the main saloon; it had been removed. He didn't sail this boat much, obviously; it was his romancing pad, Cupid's garden, and a moldy one at that. Something was wrong with the cabin sole; it looked as though it had been hacked with a hatchet; some type of plastic flooring had been glued over the original teak and holly. "I was trying to make it more modern, like" Tony explained in his high, squeaky voice. "That's Pergo."

"You installed?"

"Uh-huh."

But there were even more horrors awaiting my discovery. Sliding cabinet panels had been replaced with kitchen-type off-the-WalMart-shelf red-oak cabinet doors. There were no latches, just magnets.

"How do you keep them closed?" I asked. "How do you keep the contents of the cabinet from spilling out in a seaway?"

"In a what-way?"

I sighed. I sat down beside him on a smelly cushion next to the rickety table with a seasick-green love-candle on it, burning in a frosted jar. "Let's talk."

This was the point where Bryce now went into action. Wearing his big rubber boots, a yellow oilskin jacket, and a crushed fedora, he left us and went topside, all the while stomping around the decks above our heads, kicking hatches, stamping a little extra hard on the non-skid, deliberately taking his time, moving forward, then aft, noisily. This constantly distracted Tony, and seemed to unnerve him. He looked edgy. "What's your friend doing?" he asked, one time when he heard Bryce stomp especially hard somewhere.

"Oh, just checking things out. You know. Don't mind him."

It seems that Tony and his new second wife had acquired an older home on the lower Cape, a fashionable old place that needed some work and they'd managed to get a real deal on it. Some old-name Yankee blueblood fellow had died and they had snapped it up at a 'steal' price for what it was. Now Tony was strapped for cash and needed to raise a significant sum quickly, so that the deal wouldn't fall through. His farmhouse up in Marlborough was about to sell. He needed to turn this boat into cash and nobody seemed interested.

Bryce finally came below – saying very little but wearing a scowl – and began poking into cabinets. Trying to sound friendly, Tony asked him, "What is it you said that you do?"

"I'm retired. Live on the Vineyard" he replied, short and gruff.

Tony asked again in a little while and got the exact same answer.

"Hmm, I can see that you've got a problem under here, with the water system" Bryce noted, tersely.

"Yes, there is, not sure how bad it is, some plumbing problems I guess."

One by one, Bryce brought one issue after another to our attention, his scowl growing more severe and vinegary all the while. Finally he went back out on deck. Tony looked depressed; he lowered his head toward his folded hands.

"I'll call you in a day or so" I said. "I'm very much interested even though there are some obvious problems." Tony seemed to brighten. "I have to talk it over with my buddy up there."

"Oh sure, no problem, take your time. This is a very desirable boat, just a few small things to take care of, you know, really."

Bryce and I drove to the British Beer Company pub in West Falmouth. While the wind blew the rain in sheets outside, we washed down a late lunch of grilled bangers with a few pints of cool, sudsy ale. We discussed the boat at length.

"You had him convinced" I said. "You did a good job."

Bryce chuckled mischievously. "Hornswoggled, my boy. Did you see him, Moulie? Every time I pointed something else out, his head would hang a little bit lower, ha, ha."

"I have no idea what to offer him."

Shifting his role to mentor, Bryce replied, "Moulie, Moulie, here's what you do. Offer him a thousand dollars a foot, and a thousand dollars for good will. That's it."

I laughed. "Forty-six? That's all? He'll be insulted. He's asking sixty-nine thousand."

"Moulie, I'm telling you. That's what you should do. You know how to fill in the rest."

A day later I called Tony, and with a straight face, made my offer. "I mean, you and I both know that there are a bunch of problems. Bryce and I talked it over. As I'm sure you figured out, he's a retired marine surveyor from the Vineyard."

"Oh yes, I figured that out pretty quickly" Tony answered, a hint of resignation in his voice. "I guess he found a lot of things wrong."

The tree trunk was sawn nearly through; it was creaking, and needed only a breath more of wind to topple. I told him I'd pay him cash on the barrel. I had, after all, just sold *Privateer* a few months earlier. "To tell you the truth, I really wasn't going to accept any less than fifty" he replied, "but I guess you're right. Make it forty-six five and it's a deal."

I phoned Bryce immediately afterward "What the hell am I going to do? He accepted the offer! I couldn't believe it!"

"Now calm down, Moulie. That's just wonderful. You have some work to do, but you know what? You've got a couple of months to get her cleaned up. I can hardly wait; we're going to have a great summer!"

A couple of weeks later, just before Memorial Day, the weather suddenly changed – as it can do in these parts of New England when winter transitions to summer without the benefit of a spring in-between – and we were blessed with a week –long stretch of sunny, very warm, dry weather. While speaking on the phone to Tony, wrapping up a few last details, he remarked, disappointedly, "Cripes, with this nice weather, my phone has been ringing off the hook, all calls about the boat, all from that ad. I should have waited."

"Nah, Tony, think about it." I reassured him. "Look at it this way; you're rid of it now, it's off your back, out of your hair."

◆◆◆◆◆◆◆

Riding Out the Gale – The Return of *Mary Rose*

Great, steep seas of liquid sapphire rolled toward us in everlasting succession, lifting *Mary Rose* up, up, balancing her on their peaks, and then passing under, letting her down gently, and rolling away to leeward. Fast and busy; that was my impression of them, as though they were creatures intently focused on some urgent business somewhere far to the southward, with no time to pause or pay heed to us. Some broke briefly in curling splendor, and on such occasions, if they broke against the hull, we were showered in the cockpit with warm, sweet-salty, clean water, as thoroughly as if one had thrown buckets of seawater directly at us from only a few feet away. It was tepid and pleasant, under a brilliant sunny sky dappled with jolly white cotton-balls of cumulus clouds, and it reminded me of a day at the beach, running in the surf, but without the bright-yellow oilskin weather-repellent gear and safety harness in which I was, at the moment, attired. The ever-present roar of the wind and sea in motion filled our ears; we had to shout to be heard.

"This must be the Gulf Stream" I commented to Captain Tom. "It feels so much like it; and the color of the water…" But we feared the Stream, which was supposedly flowing in a northeasterly direction, and in opposition to the 30 knots of northwest wind that were now roiling it, stacking up the seas dangerously. Opposing northerlies make the Stream formidable; seas can become mountainous, steep, and short, and when they begin to break, a small vessel such as a cruising yacht can find itself in grave peril.

We were clawing our way northwestward from Bermuda to Newport, R.I., and the wind had been in our teeth all the way, with a big nor'easter brewing south of Nantucket. We had been battling this storm for a few days now, four of us in the 80-ft. antique wooden Herreshoff staysail schooner *Mary Rose*, on her return trip to New England for the summer, having wintered over in Tortola, BVI.

To get home, or to get anywhere back along the coast of the United States, we had to cross the northward-flowing Gulf Stream. The stream turns northeastward beginning around the latitude of Maryland, and heads off toward the British Isles. So it loomed, in my imagination, like an Atlantic Wall, blocking our way home with peril; the seas were already high; how much of a tougher time did we have in store for us ahead? There was no turning back; Bermuda was three hundred miles and more behind us. So we had decided to go westward toward the coast of Virginia, Maryland, or Delaware, since going in our chosen direction toward home was utterly impossible, and would be thus for several days yet. What little information we could obtain suggested that the storm would remain stationary for some time still, with winds out of the north, frustrating our passage home. So we sailed due west, sometimes a little more northerly when the wind shifted north or northeasterly, keeping the towering seas on the starboard bow, motor-sailing to windward under Mary Rose's two staysails only.

Captain Tom was at the helm, having taken over the watch at noon; I had been steering all morning since six, with my watchmate, Andy. I stayed in the cockpit with Tom for awhile; I was not in a mood for sleep.

"Seas must be eighteen feet," I commented to Capt. Tom.

"At the very least," he replied, and muttered a curse under his breath. "We must be in the stream. I can't imagine that it can get any worse than this!"

Sparkling, glistening, sun-drenched, blue and more blue; a terrifying beauty. It was a scene that was awe-inspiring and lovely while at the same time dangerous and without mercy. But, as the fisherman Santiago observes in The Old Man and the Sea, also without malice, after all.

I had remained in the cockpit with Captain Tom even though my watch was over, and I ought to be napping or trying to manage a bite to eat, perhaps an orange or a slice of nut-grain bread with peanut butter, but I had the nagging suspicion that we were indeed in the Gulf Stream. I remained on deck also because I was in a state of semi-rapture, I suppose; I could not stop watching the magnificence of the sea, in what Slocum once called "its grandest mood." But finally I went below with the intention of confirming or invalidating my suspicion that we had indeed entered the Gulf Stream, which can be anywhere from ten to twenty miles across.

I had brought my notebook computer along, loaded with a chart-plotter software program and a GPS antenna device that plugged into the computer. Once it picked up the satellite signal, and I zoomed the chart in, the program indicated that our position was right smack-dab in the middle of the Stream, positioned on the 'estimated axis' of the Gulf Stream. I breathed a sigh of relief, and passed the word around. "Well that's good news," Captain Tom said. "We're doing all right, right now. If we can get through this, we'll probably be fine the rest of the way." Indeed; after a short nap, I awoke again at watch-time, at nearly six in the evening, and emerged on deck to an entirely different scene; the water was dark green and there was a distinct chill in the air. It was the North Atlantic that I was used to, a half hour before sunset. "We're out of the Gulf Stream," Captain Tom announced. From this point, I thought, there is nothing in our way; let it blow. We're getting used to it, and the boat can take it.

Now, it stands to reason that a man who has stepped inadvertently into a bucket of fish-offal will henceforth be more mindful of where he puts his feet when walking down a dock, with the intention of avoiding the repetition of such a mishap. But can you fathom a man deliberately stepping back into that same bucket the next time he walks the dock? And do so with enthusiasm, and deliberately so, at that? This is what the person who does not love the sea cannot understand about the sailor. To him or her, the bucket of offal and going to sea are one and the same. But why would an intelligent fellow who has experienced a rough ocean passage readily sign up to endure the same ordeal again only a few months later? Because he or she is a sailor, of course, and will not only repeat the experience of being tossed about in a small boat in the middle of the vast ocean once, or twice, but moreover will repeat the same again and again and again. I thought about this as I lay in my berth in the darkness, trying to hang on, trying to grab a moment of sleep as the *Mary Rose* slammed about noisily in stormy seas, and occasional droplets of cold water, seeping through the deck, dripped onto my face or into my eyes, or wetted my pillow and blanket. Here I am again, I thought; I shook my head in bewilderment, and quite nearly laughed at myself; incredibly, I realized, I was in exactly the same pickle barrel as I had been this past November, only now in even worse circumstances. And I had told myself, at the end of my November passage on *Mary Rose* to Tortola, that I would be most reluctant to ever again embark upon such an uncomfortable misadventure! Now why in the hell, I queried my conscience, had I signed up for this trip, and with an eagerness that bordered upon frenzy? It seemed to be the very stuff of madness. As the wind topped and exceeded fifty knots during the night, I thought, well, you fool, you've done it now, you came back for more, and got a full ration of what you had before plus some. Now you've no choice but to ride it out, and make the best of it. But as every silver lining has a cloud, so the obverse is true; at least my stomach was the least of my worries. I might find myself adrift in a raft, but my own hold would be well stowed; after the second day out from Bermuda, I'd acquired my sea-legs, and no amount of motion of the boat, no matter how violent, had upset it since.

The *Mary Rose* had sailed to Tortola, BVI, by way of Bermuda, in late November. I had been aboard for that stormy trip south. She had spent the winter cruising the Caribbean, topping it off by sailing in Antigua's Classic Yacht Regatta and taking home an award. But when it came time for the springtime trip back north to Newport and Bristol, I had not been called; I was disappointed, but I understood; a one-way air ticket to Tortola from New England is an expensive proposition and the Captain was on a tight budget. A young fellow from Maine, seeking passage north, signed on. I knew when they left, and I followed them with my chart-plotter in dead reckoning mode. It turns out that they arrived in Bermuda only three hours earlier than my ETA for them!

But in Bermuda, the sailor from Maine left. He'd had a rough time of it with seasickness, and was not willing to continue on. Airplane turbulence was as much now as he had stomach for. On a Sunday morning, two days after they had arrived, I received a call on my cell phone. It was Captain Tom. "So, Mike, are you busy?" He laughed. I was on a plane the next morning, on a remarkably short – 90-minute – flight out of Boston. Once the young man from Maine had left, there were only three remaining to take the boat home, across 630 miles of open North Atlantic. Captain Tom, his lady Bonnie, and crewman Andy. Andy was the only sailor familiar with the boat other than Tom and capable of working the foredeck. So there were not enough sailors aboard, and thus I was summoned to rejoin the crew, and no one, I felt, could be more delighted than I at the prospect of sailing on *Mary Rose* once more!

There were many boats in Bermuda, and five times as many sailors, seemingly bottled up, itching to be on their way, but a continuous pattern of bad weather had kept them in port. Two boats left the day I arrived, and returned the next day, battered and beat up. Some said it would be more than a week before anyone could safely leave. But our captain had his doubts; the forecast days ahead was nothing if not vague; but it suggested that the low that had driven those boats back in was passing well off to the east. Yet oddly this had been an off year; a succession of lows had moved like a parade across the U.S. from the Pacific, developing into gale centers in the North Atlantic. The jet stream was off, some said. But after mulling it over, our captain decided that the outlook was favorable enough to go, and it looked that way to me, too.

The night before we left, we attended a lively party at the home of a local sailmaker. Many cruisers were there, and it was a wonderful evening of wine, hors d'oeuvres, and camaraderie among sailors, long-distance passagemakers, and cruising lifestyle people. If you are one of them, or even doing such a thing as making a deepwater passage in a sailboat for the first time, you will find only friends in that gathering; and even if you are acquainted with no one, you will still find a willing ear, a friendly voice, and an outstretched hand of welcome. And although we sailed out of sunny St. George's the next afternoon to friendly cheers and waving hands, I heard much later on that there were not a few among them who felt that we were earnestly out of our minds to be leaving when we did.

The morning that we crossed the Gulf Stream, I went topside with my cup of tea in hand, to begin my watch with Andy, just before six o'clock, to find the wind light and the seas moderate. The sun was up but it was behind a low layer of dark clouds. The air was warm and moist; in the distance, beneath the dark clouds, cone-shaped funnel clouds were trying to form in a couple of different places. "Waterspouts!" I exclaimed, and cursed; another hazard to look out for. The sea was purple beneath the clouds, and the thought passed through my mind that perhaps we were in a warm eddy of the Stream, or approaching the Stream itself. Little did I know that we would be in it by mid-day, with winds piping up to thirty knots plus and seas building to blue hills.

We had seen so many Portuguese Man-of-War jellyfish that I could only imagine that millions upon millions dotted the seas beyond the scope of our vision. Indeed, they were everywhere, deadly iridescent blue bubbles that looked at first like partially inflated plastic sandwich bags floating on the surface. We had seen dolphins, flying fish, and a couple of large, slow, green creatures beneath the surface that might have been sea turtles or ocean sunfish. A gray-skinned whale surfaced briefly near the boat once, and another did, unseen, but we smelled his dank, fishy, malodorous breath when we passed over the spot where he had just been before sounding. Occasionally, a white-tailed tropicbird circled for a little while overhead.

The sea is a painter's canvas, and light is the artist. It is not dull, nor empty, nor simply water and sky, but an ever-changing tapestry, always different, always refreshing itself. Clouds change the way light paints the sea and sky; they change color and texture, sometimes dramatically and sometimes with great subtlety. But it is no still-life; always in motion, it is a performing art.

But the interpretation of the masterpiece is done by the mind and the imagination. Where there is nothing familiar, the mind struggles to add it. Sometimes I have felt as though land was near, or that a reflection of light from an instrument was, in the corner of my eye, a marshy shore off the coast of Virginia. But most remarkably, one night as we sailed through a strange moonless night with clouds stacked at different levels of the sky and occasional heat lightning, I could have sworn that we were sailing through a dark forest of impossibly tall pines, or redwoods, on either side, rather than hundreds of miles from the nearest coast. And two nights later, in the midst of the gale, spray blew across the *Mary Rose's* foredeck, illuminated by the surreal green glow of the starboard sidelight. It was a plunging, lashing, spray-whipped vision of water traveling horizontally athwartships as *Mary Rose* beat strongly and doggedly to windward, powerfully, unstoppably. I watched this unlivable no-man's land of the foredeck through the clear panel of the savagely shaking pram-hood dodger. Ship against the sea, challenging, persevering, taking a beating in the process.

We could not get home along our chosen course. Thus, in a few days we sailed exhaustedly into Cape May, N.J., to dry out the boat and take on fuel and to rest. Two days later, in much better conditions, we steamed northeast on a beeline for Block Island and arrived in cold, gray, windy Bristol Harbor after nearly 19 hours of motorsailing. It felt good to stand on the pier in my own town again, next to all things familiar, home, family, and little dog. And, once again, I stood in awe of the antique wooden vessel that had carried us home, kept us alive, and had survived a rough sea and a nasty gale. I had to go home, but I could not but pause for a few moments to look back at her, suddenly and oddly emotional, with feelings of deep affection. And I then understood what it has meant, for centuries, for a sailor to be attached to a ship. You cannot explain it, but you know it when you experience it.

The nor'easter we sailed into didn't have a name, but it had an eye, and back home, our families watched in horror as the thing developed and unfolded on the evening news reports on television. We saw winds in excess of 50 knots, days with the winds between 35 and 40 knots, unrelenting, unrelenting. Two vessels sank; one a hundred miles south of Nantucket, another one somewhere out off New York, their crews rescued by the Coast Guard. At the time of this writing, it is now midsummer and Mary Rose rides contentedly on her mooring in Bristol Harbor, enjoying the kind attention of Andy's skilled varnish brush and patient care. Where she will cruise to next, one can only guess!

◆◆◆◆◆◆◆

Flying fish

One of the many wondrous things that one reads about, in books and stories about long ocean passages in small boats, is the appearance of flying fish. I first saw them many years ago while serving on a Coast Guard ship in the Gulf of Mexico; I saw them again many years later, while sailing a 45-foot catamaran to the Caribbean island of St. Martin, on a boat delivery, with my friend Stan.

I had read about flying fish, and how the old circumnavigators would hang a lantern in the shrouds at night to attract them. They would leap aboard during the night, where they could be found on deck in the morning and fried for breakfast. Fresh fish for breakfast! Had not Capt. Joshua Slocum so sumptuously taken his morning meal, at his ease? I had heard also that they are quite delicious, so it was with some real surprise – perhaps a little apprehension at first – that I heard a flying-fish come slapping aboard during the middle of the night, during my 11 to 2 watch on board the cat heading south.

It was a stormy, wet night, as were so many of these miserable nights on our passage from New York. Not rainy, mind you, but overcast and stormy, windy and with spray blowing aboard, and as black as pitch outside. The big cat heaved and banged and slammed its way across the seas, the nice wooden panels of the cabin sole predictably popping up with the blows from below, and the dinette tables jumping and shrugging with undisguised rage and infernal clatter of their wooden extensions and folded parts.

Now take a moment to envision this; imagine the wild, wet, windy, evening of an autumn storm, driving gusts of rain and occasional soaking showers, and how good it feels to quickly step inside of your house and shut the door, closing it all out, to retire to your comfortable bed. Doesn't it feel cozy to shut out the blast? Yet the irony of this thought occurred to me, after going out to the cockpit to check the sails, speed, and course, as I ducked back into the main cabin and shut the sliding-glass cabin door to the cockpit behind me. I could not, as at home, shut out the wind, rain, and storm! That was an illusion! Rather, I was borne upon it, at its whim and mercy, bouncing across the cobble-sea in this tiny coracle, in the midst of the storm, barely sheltered from it. It was a sobering thought.

On one previous such night a few days before, so far at sea, I had managed to repair the generator (genset), so that we could operate the autopilot at night. Now I conducted most of my watch from the dry relative comfort of the cabin, keeping my lookout through the window ports, and going on deck only occasionally to check the heading and the sails and to ensure that all was well. On one such occasion, as I opened the glass door to the weather, I heard an odd flapping sound coming from the cockpit, which at first alarmed me slightly, since my mind was weary and sleepy. But I soon woke fully and found the source of the sound, a flying fish that had just come aboard, and was trying desperately to find the sea once again.

I picked up the fish and looked at it in the dim light; it was beautiful, bluish-silvery, with big transparent fin-wings and large saucer-eyes, so much the better for seeing at night. You will perhaps be pleased to know that breakfast was far from my mind at that point. Indeed, my reverence for the sea, and wariness, now, after what I had seen it capable of, left me with no desire to take the life of this little fish. Bordering on superstition, my thoughts were that if I took its life needlessly, then perhaps bad luck would come upon the boat as retribution from the old Ocean herself. So, with a thought in mind to placate the Ocean and earn merit and mercy, perhaps, I happily tossed the creature back into the sea, musing, like the fox that eyed the grapes, that it was indeed to small and bony a fish to bother cooking, anyway. Later, I did find a sizable one on the foredeck of the port pontoon, but it had baked in the sun for a couple of days and was hardly palatable. I also found one in the bilge of the dinghy on the stern, bloatedly floating around in sloshing warm, brackish rainwater, obviously dead for a couple of days and well beyond hopes of cooking. So much for the anticipated meal of flying fish. One of my fondest memories of these fish, though, comes from years ago, in the Gulf of Mexico, as our Coast Guard ship sliced through the shimmering turquoise waters of sunny afternoons well off the Texas coast. Entire schools of flying fish – droves of them – constantly rose from the sea in front of the bow, to cruise on the wind for a hundred feet or more across the sparkling blue tropical swells before plunging back through the surface. They would emerge from the water, their flapping fins suddenly frozen motionless, shining and gossamer in the sun like cellophane, outstretched fully, then flutter once, twice again, then freeze, then dive into the warm seas. I stood on the deck transfixed and watched them, never tiring of doing so.

◆◆◆◆◆◆◆

Engines, Angels, and the Meaning of Luck

I'm not much for silly fads and new-age stuff – the whole concept of angels, for instance – but if there are angels, and if a good angel is watching over me, he earned his grog the other day when my old blue Perkins diesel blew.

Many people believe in angels. When I was a child, I was taught that each of us has a guardian angel assigned to watch over us, particularly our souls, though it was never clear to me which of the two the angel was charged with protecting specifically. As a youngster I actually preferred that, if I had such an angel, he or she would concentrate more on keeping me out of physical harm's way, and the soul, for all practical purposes, could go to hell.

I think the whole angel concept is a fine idea but have often felt (for reasons that I do not choose to explain here) that my angel is of the lower-pay-grade kind, maybe even the variety with horns. Or, if I have a good angel, he or she is either asleep most of the time, or belongs to a union that happens to be in perpetua in a heavenly work slowdown or strike.

All such doubts about the quality and competence of my angel were dispelled, however, when my boat's old 4-banger diesel auxiliary decided to sputter and die. Yes, I was under way. But in truth, there could have been few more auspicious times for the engine to fail unless it had been, for example, on a test-bench. This is why I am now a firm believer in angels. Mine finally woke up and came through in a pinch. He kept my engine alive just long enough for me to make it to my mooring.

My angel's performance oddly reminded me of an old friend, Jason, who used to fly a great deal in his sales engineering job for the company that we worked for. Jason was a bright guy but he was also a bit of a smart-aleck. He was fascinated by air travel and commercial flight, which was fortunate because his job required him to spend so much time in the air. He used to like to hobnob with the pilots and once asked a pilot why, with so much automated guidance – planes practically taking off and landing by themselves – that pilots were needed at all, and might even be overpaid, given the nearly 'hands off' nature of their job in flight. The pilot cracked a smile, and replied. "Well, because every so often – and it may only be once in a great while – I have to step in and save your ass. Now isn't that worth it?"

Now, after a miserably stormy summer in New England – and we have been praying for the long-absent Bermuda High that used to be a commonplace weather pattern here in summer – the forecaster promised that one would be settling in over the northeast. That meant sunny days, steady winds, all for a stretch of nearly a week. Bonanza!

I was thinking of heading out in a day or so and inviting along any of my ol' pirate crew of fellows who might want a berth on this floating spirits locker, to cruise to Nantucket, Block Island, or the Elizabeth Islands up in Buzzard's Bay.

Planning in advance, I brought my old Gulfstar sloop to the marina dock for the weekend, tidying up, cleaning, and preparing the boat for a cruise of three days or more. On Tuesday morning, it was time to leave the dock – I had used up my allotted time – and since I was still a couple of days away from going cruising, I decided to bring the boat around the Bristol peninsula to her alternate mooring in the Kickemuit River, off Mount Hope Bay. Motoring leisurely, it's an hour trip, no more. The boat had not been in the Kikky at all this season and I thought it would be nice to have her moored there for a couple of days. That mooring is near my house, and there is a right-of-way at the bottom of a nearby street where I keep a dinghy pulled up on the hard.

The water was flat, with a slight westerly breeze; it was a beautiful, warm summer morning. The engine seemed to be running fine, but as always, I was babying her. I had purchased this boat four years earlier, at a reduced price, knowing that it was a "project" boat. Her Achilles' heel was her engine; an old four-cylinder Perkins 4-108 that dated from the day the boat was built in 1986. It was 22 years old now, never having been rebuilt, with no hour meter; I estimated that it had perhaps a million hours on it, if it had a fortnight. Still, it ran fairly steadily and did not belch black smoke or knock unless one tried to make her work too hard – such as advance beyond 1/3 throttle – so I kept oil in her, since she oozed and burned a little, and I kept water and antifreeze in the coolant tank even though the blow-by from the pistons (or failed head gasket) kept exhaust bubbling out of the coolant reservoir and there was black oil in the coolant tank floating on top all the time. I had been told by a mechanic back when I bought the boat that the floating oil "was not a good sign." But again, that was a few years back.

Now I was entering the narrow, twisting mouth of the

Kickemuit River. I came around the last corner of the S-curve and saw my mooring buoy and pickup stick, or tall-boy, dead ahead. The tide was still incoming and the gentle current and light breezes were right behind me.

I was 50 yards from the mooring buoy when the engine blew.

A few minutes earlier, the engine had begun doing something unusual – slowing down, fluctuating in speed. It never had done that before. Problems came to mind – clogged fuel filter, pinhole air leak in the fuel line – but before I had the chance to do much more thinking, the engine began making nasty knocking noises, and then it quit. I restarted her once, but she ran only for a few moments. Then she would not turn over at all.

Old auxiliary diesel engines are a lot like old married guys, those of us who have 25 years-plus hitched to the old wagon. They work hard all the time, say very little (because complaining is useless) and then just die, all of a sudden, without any real warning, and all that's left is a whiff of the stink of burnt oil.

The boat still had some way on, so I coasted right up to the tall-boy and grabbed the pennant and secured my boat.

How nice that I recently had a new 500-pound mushroom anchor put down there and new top chain, good enough to ride out a hurricane. Now I'll get the use out of it, I thought. Now I'll get my money's worth. Isn't that the way it always happens – if you're lucky?

Oddly enough the engine had not given any sign of overheating, and cooling water was still pumping from the exhaust before she died, so I had no idea what the problem was when she began acting oddly. Now it seemed (after it quit) very hot and I could smell something burning, like dirty engine oil. I pulled off some panels and noticed that one of the bilge compartments – not the one that drains to the bilge pump, thankfully –was full of all my engine oil. Don't know how it got there, did not see a point of egress or an obvious leak from the port side of the engine. Somehow it escaped, sump ran dry, engine seized. That's all she wrote. I realized that the engine had been on life support for four years anyway, and didn't owe me anything. But I think like what I am, a Yankee; if bolts still hold the damned thing together, and some of them are shiny on the heads where the paint has flaked off, then by golly it ought to be running. But engines need oil to keep running. I knew that my engine used some oil but I knew the rate and always added some after motoring for an afternoon. In this case, even after very little running it all got out, something must have failed.

In some ways I am relieved; I had been waiting for the axe to fall. But what kind of luck is that for the old gal to give up the ghost 50 yards from the mooring, coming in sweetly, instead of in trouble on a lee shore or 16 miles west of Block Island in a calm? Or trying to negotiate a narrow and unforgiving channel stemming a tide? I wonder if I have any luck left in the bank, for I used a good sum of it that morning.

So the engine is dead but at least the boat is safe on her mooring. She will have to be sailed away, anywhere she goes; but that's not so bad. After all, Joshua Slocum sailed around the world alone in *Spray* with no engine at all. A sloop is very maneuverable even in light airs under just the mainsail. I'm afraid, though, that *RagBagger's* 2008 cruising season is basically over. In the months ahead, I can stay aboard, like the boat-bums who live on the motorless hulks permanently moored in Key West's backwaters. I have a grill to cook my burgers, and a cooler to keep the beer cold. My water tanks are full; the wind generator makes enough power to keep the batteries up if I use electricity sparingly.

It just might be fun for awhile, while I save up for that replacement engine!

◆◆◆◆◆◆◆

Farewell to Captain Slocum

"To young men contemplating a voyage I would say go...Dangers there are, to be sure...but the intelligence and skill God gives to man reduce these to a minimum...You must then know the sea, and know that you know it, and not forget that it was made to be sailed over."
- Capt. Joshua Slocum, 'Sailing Alone Around the World'.

November 14, 2009 was a rainy, gray, dark, leafless, blowy day, the kind of day that makes one want to hoist sail and head south for the winter. It was also the 100th anniversary of the last time that Capt. Joshua Slocum, the first person to sail around the world alone, was last seen alive.

It's an odd anniversary because it is the last anniversary of any kind to do with Slocum that falls within the century mark. After this, regardless of the meaninglessness of dates, days or years following one after another, there is the sense that a boundary has been crossed. Slocum is now, I suppose, truly gone, adrift among old books, statistics, and sepia-toned photographs from another age; a certain finality descends on the legend and last mystery of Captain Joshua Slocum. He's as gone as he ever has been since 1909, but somehow, it seems, he and Spray have finally disappeared beyond the horizon.

According to Slocum's great biographer, Walter Teller, Slocum was declared dead (it took some years for Slocum's second wife Hettie to get it officially declared – even until 1924) as of November 14, 1909, the day that he officially set sail from Martha's Vineyard for the last time with the intention of exploring the Amazon and Orinoco rivers. He was never seen or heard from again. He set out in his aging craft in a rising gale, as he had every fall for a few years, headed for the Caribbean and southern waters to avoid, he used to joke, the expense of having to purchase a winter coat. More probably, he didn't like New England winters or the prospect of being cooped up for months inside in close quarters with Hettie. No doubt Hettie felt the same way about being cooped up with him.

Slocum was 51 years old when he left on his history-making voyage in 1895 – and 51 was not 'young' in those days. Some might say that even today it is not especially young. Now, at 53, I can say that Captain Slocum has been part of my life since my childhood; so it was with some odd sense of personal loss that I marked the 100th anniversary of Slocum's disappearance.

When I was a boy, I read everything that I could get my hands on that was about the sea. This was because I spent so much time on the water with my younger cousin Dan and our grandfather. Grandpa was a boatbuilder, sailor, fisherman, water-man, and a member of Bristol's little old-Yankee yacht club; he was also semi-retired, so in the summer time, we spent many days down at the Club and out on the bay with Grandpa, putting around in skiffs, fishing, sailing, and getting ourselves suntanned and salt-crusted. We spent more time in those days with Grandpa than without own fathers, at least in the summer when school was out. This was not the fault of our fathers, who were hard-working men putting in long hours to earn a living for their families in the mid-1960s. But Grandpa was a wonderful and patient man who knew all the things that young boys like to do, from building forts in the rocky shore-line to exploring the shores of Hog Island, and he indulged us end-lessly in those things while encouraging our imaginations to roam. If a boy is lucky enough to be raised by, or spend a great deal of time with, a grandfather, then he will be blessed by that experience for the rest of his life. So I wanted to grow up to be very much like Grandpa if I could.

The ladies in the Public Library always knew what section and shelves I would be visiting when I came in the door. I made a bee-line for the books about the sea; I discovered the wonderful world of the 'Vagrant Viking', Peter Freuchen; I became enthralled by the Bounty trilogy, and the strange allure of the tropics, which, to a New-England boy hiking through winter slush in his galoshes and overcoat, seemed the very vision of Paradise. I eagerly followed the adventures of Robin Lee Graham as he sailed Dove around the world single-handedly, in real time, in 1965. Grandpa and Grandma subscribed to *National Geographic*, and I followed the older boy's adventures from month to month; he became a current-day hero to me, someone whose path I could follow, too. Indeed, I once took a world map out of National Geographic, and marked it up, tracing a route in pencil around the world, a voyage that I would make in my imaginary sailboat, Resolution (I had been reading a book about Captain Cook).

One day, in elementary school reading class, we were introduced to a new scholastic program designed to encourage us to read. Once a week we would read a folding card that had an excerpt in it from a different famous book, and then we would write answers to essay questions about what we had read. The excerpts were tantalizing, for the most part, and they had been designed to be that way. But on one occasion I read an excerpt that riveted me. It was about a man who, many years ago, had sailed around the world alone, and had been the first to do so; I recognized the name from the Robin Lee Graham's accounts in *National Geographic* – Capt. Joshua Slocum. But what caught my attention was Slocum's account of speaking orders to his 'crew', and then answering them himself; and how the crew never, of course, had any complaints for the cook! I decided that I had to find that book at the library – *Sailing Alone Around the World.* I found it, certainly, and what followed was a lifelong adventure, a one-way friendship if you will, an obsession, a fascination, as I first sailed with Slocum on his boat *Spray* around the world, and then repeated the adventure, over the years, again and again.

Growing up with Slocum was an interesting experience. You cannot know Slocum in any different a manner than anyone can know a person no longer physically living. On top of that, Slocum was and is, in his literature, a master of controlling just how well he wants us to know him. He pays out slack in that line slowly, in a measured way, always in control. He isn't stingy, nor is he careless; and now that he is gone, the body of knowledge will never change, and perhaps he is comfortable with that, wherever he is.

But the Slocum persona fascinated me. I grew up with Sailing Alone, and the folklore that goes along with everything Slocum. One wintry Saturday, Grandpa was driving Dan and me down through Tiverton, R.I., and over into Westport, Mass. – lovely farm country down by the sea, a favorite place of Grandpa's to take us for a drive when we boys were feeling restless on a sleety, cold afternoon and needed to get out of the house. Across a potato-field and pasture, down near the Seapowet Marsh, there stood, out in the middle of a cow pasture, a magnificent tall oak tree, with a great trunk – perhaps 150 years old – all by itself, exposed to the gales blowing in off the ocean and the Sakonnet River. "Look," I exclaimed to Grandpa, "There it is – a pasture oak, just like the one Captain Slocum cut Spray's new keel from."

Anyone who has read *Sailing Alone* understands the virtues of the pasture oak, because it stands alone unprotected by any other trees around it, it grows strong and sinewy, tough and worthy of being cut for a keel. Thus did Captain Slocum's lore and teaching infuse my life. The tree, by the way, still stands, remarkably; and even now, when I drive down along that route, I think of Slocum; and when I have driven my kids by there, I have explained its significance to them, but I have to speak loudly to get past their ear buds and the sounds that the little electronic music players are blasting into their ears. They give me quizzical looks, and roll their eyes.

I often dreamed of following in Slocum's wake – as many others have done, since – but always feared that I might not be up to the task. My mother told me that it was impossible – that I could never do it, that I was not mentally stable enough. And who doubts their mother's word, when they are a youngster? But in the years since then, I have met many solo circumnavigators, which opened my eyes quite a bit; they are a special bunch all right, and I have come to realize that on a solo circumnavigation, total sanity might be a liability, not an asset. Cynics like my mother might point to the example of poor Donald Crowhurst, who went insane and reportedly committed suicide during the Golden Globe around-the-world race. But to those doubters I would say that Captain Crowhurst reportedly left England a sane man; to survive a solo circumnavigation, you have to be a little barmy before you leave, and every solo circumnavigator I have ever met has appeared, to me, to have always marched to a different drummer.

The key, though, as Slocum reminds us, in a strong, clear voice, is knowledge, preparedness, confidence in oneself, and faith in God. A sound ship, of course, is a great help too. But in *Sailing Alone*, Slocum summarizes, and encourages. His words, over time, blow the fear out of our souls the same way that a brisk, cold northerly wind under a deep sapphire sky on an October morning blows the stagnancy out of the sea air and refreshes the heart and mind:

"To young men contemplating a voyage I would say go...Dangers there are, to be sure...but the intelligence and skill God gives to man reduce these to a minimum...You must then know the sea, and know that you know it, and not forget that it was made to be sailed over."

Capt. Joshua Slocum belongs to another age; but like the endless wash of surf on the shore, Slocum's story and message of the unconquerable human spirit, and the possibilities inherent in it, is timeless, if not always in vogue with the times. It is about what a man can do, with naught but his knowledge, his faith, his ingenuity and self-reliance; and what we admire most about Slocum is that whatever befalls him, he finds a way to be cheerful about it, or philosophical, or even amused. He never complains or whines. He never sets himself above us, but instead tells us that what he has achieved, we can also achieve, if we will only apply ourselves and rely on our inner strengths. Is it any wonder, then, that Captain Slocum continues to inspire, 100 years later, small-boat solo circumnavigations of the globe? Captain Slocum and Spray have been gone for a century now; but for all true sailors, and young men and women who dream of adventure, he is very much alive; and best of all, he was kind enough to leave us his charts. All we need do is follow.

◆◆◆◆◆◆◆

Perils of 'Nautical Cuisine'

I'll never understand where the concept of "nautical cuisine" originated. I've always thought of it as a contradiction in terms; e.g., "jumbo shrimp." But nowadays we read about it all the time in boating magazines; somehow 'nautical cuisine' has become an accepted fact. But if nautical cuisine is so great, why does it seem that so many skippers and crews can hardly wait to go ashore to eat, practically as soon as they tie up in their destination harbor?

I have going-cruising cookbooks that I have never opened, much less followed a recipe from. Many of them call for ingredients that can be (supposedly) readily found in a boat's galley cabinets, such as "a can of condensed tomato soup." I won't eat anything that calls for a can of condensed tomato soup as an ingredient. It reminds me too much of the way my sainted grandmother used to cook. And I certainly will not carry such a doleful item as a can of tomato soup aboard, lest I be stuck somewhere a great distance from land with nothing else to eat but that can of soup. I would rather make a salad of the sea-grass growing on my rudder-post.

Is there any tradition – really – of fine cuisine being served aboard boats, or is it a common myth that has simply acquired credibility during modern times? Worse, has the false concept of 'nautical cuisine' been shamelessly promoted by cruising magazines? Perhaps crew and guests in a bygone era ate lovely dinners aboard their splendid steam-yachts during the Victorian age. But by and large, today's cruising boats – power and sail – are too small and too stuffy for truly elegant meal preparation, and there is hardly enough cabinet or cooler space to store the range and quantity of ingredients really necessary for refined multiple course meals.

The cooler, or icebox, is a good example supporting my assertion. Unless your main course is beer for every evening's dinner (and I know some cruisers for whom that is the daily staple, an ongoing meal commencing somewhere after 10 o'clock in the forenoon) there will not be much room for anything else in there.

Consider for a moment the awful stuff that the old-time sailors ate, dreadful fare that was hardly haute cuisine; Even Jimmy Buffett opines for a cheeseburger in one of his songs. But excluding mega-yacht owners – who really aren't proper water men anyway, since they probably cannot even smell the sea from their maxi-yacht bridge wings - sailors, or 'blow-boat' men, by and large, have no tradition of eating well aboard. Even in the peacock days of the great racing J-boats, when not a spare ounce of weight was carried below, such vessels as Resolute or Columbia, with old Captain Nat Herreshoff or Charlie Barr at the helm, no one ate very much of anything, I would wager. There was certainly no great cast-iron Shipmate coal-burning galley belowdecks. The poor Norwegian crewmembers probably had to sneak smoked dried herring and hard crackers aboard in their pockets, enough to last for a day's racing off Newport or Sandy Hook. I have never read of Captain 'Nat' eating anything but cornmeal johnnycakes; indeed he probably actually never ate anything else, being a parsimonious, tough old skate.

When my wife Denise and I first owned a boat that was (at long last) too large to row, the first thing we wanted to do in the way of eating aboard was to prepare nice dinners for ourselves and our guests. It seemed so novel, so new, and so yachty. But we learned quickly that preparing complicated meals in the galley is neither practical nor fun. First, since we generally go boating in the warmer months, when firing up the galley, and especially the oven, makes the confined space below unbearably hot, even with all the hatches open. Then we discovered that there were simply not enough burners to prepare everything at once, and keep it all hot, while waiting to serve. Lastly, when cleanup time came – well, the cabin was festooned with drying dishes and drying dish towels; it looked a little like Laundry Day in the Bronx. And, of course, it was no fun. It took five times longer than preparing a simple meal at home.

So we have learned our lessons:

Lesson #1: The galley is for coffee, almost exclusively. If you get up early enough in the morning, before the day gets hot, you can make eggs and bacon, sausage, toast, and whatever else. This is fine, because the first meal of the day should be a very hearty one. All subsequent meals are beer, which of course does not require the use of the galley at all. But the first use of the galley every morning is to make copious pots of coffee. This does not heat the cabin up appreciably and it doesn't matter anyhow because most of the crew have crawled up on deck to get some fresh air, and to gradually wink the goo out of their eyes. This type of activity usually follows a very late night at The Roaring Pirate tavern ashore.

Lesson #2: Never try to cook while under way. I don't care if the stove has gimbals; it doesn't matter, everything will go, as my friend Bruce quotes Don Street, "galley west." You might pull it off if motoring in a calm; but you're better off nibbling crackers and cheese and blowing the frost off another cerveza.

Lesson #3: God's three main gifts to sailors are fair winds, following seas, and the rail-mounted barbecue grill. If you are going to cook at all aboard, grill, grill everything that you can, either on the grill itself or in a pan on top of the grill, for such as eggs. With a properly-designed covered grill (and I prefer the charcoal burning type, using 'cowboy' charcoal and hickory chips) one can grill delightful steaks, chicken, and other animal parts and even char some vegetables or kabobs and never have a pan to wash. There will be no heat, odor, or smoke below. Ashes and smoke all blow astern – when riding on a mooring or anchor, or motoring to windward. Again, if cooking or grilling under way, Rule #2 applies, e.g., don't.

I recall one summer morning's trip back from Block Island – a late morning crossing from the Block to Point Judith – leisurely sailing downwind in light airs and nearly calm seas. I had the silly idea that it would be sensible to light the grill and cook some chicken drumsticks en route; after all, we would be out there for the balance of the day.

The little drumsticks were doing charmingly well – golden-brown and crispy with a heavenly aroma - and were just seconds from being ready to eat when a ferry wake took me by surprise as I was turning them for the last time. While thus distracted, as I grasped the rail to steady myself, I watched helplessly as a juicy, plump, sizzling drumstick – the best of the lot – danced across the grill, did a gentle roll, curtseyed, and then pirouetted off the stern and – I swear it hissed as it hit the water – plunged more than a dozen fathoms to the bottom of Block Island Sound. I can still hear the happy little sun-speckled ripples of the Sound laughing at me as I cursed a blue streak. I had tasted that little drumstick already in my mind two seconds before it did its own version of the Patagonian Cliff-Dive.

Yet there are times when I actually have eaten well aboard, but always with the help of the grill, and grilling on a boat can rise to the level of exquisite art. Such occasions are more the exception than the rule, however, but here is one memorable example.

One cool, breezy Memorial Day weekend at the end of May, my salty, grizzled Liverpudlian friend Paul and I went cruising on *RagBagger* to Block Island. An Englishman loves his lamb, and so

94

do I, so we had brought a couple of frenched racks of lamb along, intending to grill them, and the racks were already seasoned liberally with cracked pepper, rosemary, Herbs de Provence, and garlic, and left to marinate in the cooler, nestled cozily between tall pint cans of Old Speckled Hen. We cruised downwind from Narragansett Bay with a fresh, sturdy nor'wester and picked up a mooring in New Harbor. It was a cold weekend, but blue and bright; there weren't many boats in the harbor on guest moorings, and those that were there had clustered in the mooring area near the town dock, which, coincidentally, is right next to a favorite tap and restaurant. It was very windy out of the north, and the evening before, after tying up, we had gone ashore in our dinghy to slake our thirsts and had, unfortunately, tarried a bit late. I remember rowing back to the boat in the darkness with good Paul seated in the stern-sheets roaring out "Heart of Oak" to the harbor, and another tune I don't remember, something about Lord Nelson's arm, or short-arm, some time after midnight.

But now it was Sunday morning and the sun was up and the wind was brisk and we sat in the cockpit with our coffee feeling a bit hungry. For some odd reason, the Oldport Launch wasn't running yet, maybe because it was Sunday, or early in the season, and we did not feel like rowing ashore in the harbor chop and then hiking all the way to the village for an egg, so I went aft to the grill, filled it full of cowboy charcoal, and fired it up.

Now remember that to a hungry person, or to carnivorous hungry people in general, a charcoal grill firing up smells pretty nice even when nothing is yet cooking in it. It causes one to sniff the air and salivate; the belly starts to grumble. It has, I think, something to do with primordial instinct, wood smoke, and the Old Brain. Beyond that I cannot explain in depth, as that is where my real knowledge of the subject ends. But as the tricky, puffy norther blew around the harbor, all of the boats tended to swing about, which gave everyone downwind of us, within the range of a generous arc, a lovely morning whiff of a charcoal grill lighting up.

I rigged the Bimini top and set the cockpit table, and Paul and I settled into the center-cockpit of my dear old bleach-bottle Gulfstar sloop, affectionately known as "Old Spider-web". In this position we were quite visible, especially to surrounding boats, as we hoisted the day's first generous goblets of rich red Cabernet, and ate the first crackers smeared with the ripe old blue Stilton that Paul had brought back with him from a recent trip home over the pond. I put the lamb on the grill, and threw in some hickory chips; fragrant smoke billowed astern. I had a loaf of bread baking in the galley oven below, and the baked-bread smell wandered up the hatch and was carried aft to mingle with the grilling lamb aroma and hickory smoke.

I suddenly noticed – and am not sure how I had missed it, really – a rather fancy Hunter yacht of nearly the same size as our old crate, perhaps a few feet longer, moored nearby – actually adjacent to us, off the port quarter. It was a well-appointed cutter yacht with expensive modern rigging, a mirror-shiny Navy-blue hull, first class in every respect. As the wind swung the boats around in the densely packed mooring field, sometimes they appeared nearly alongside, then swung off astern. Every now and then, the fragrant smoke of our barbecue wafted o'er their dodger and cockpit. I saw that there were two people aboard – a hairy-chested self-important-looking man and certainly his straw-blond wife, both appeared to be in their forties. They were sitting in the cockpit – I didn't see a dinghy, so I assumed that they were dependent upon the launch, which was not yet running, to get ashore – doing nothing. They were eating nothing, drinking nothing, maybe just waiting. I had no idea why they were just sitting there, perhaps that was the husband's idea of relaxing on a long weekend. But they seemed alone together on the boat. The man looked grumpy, staring ahead through his shades, stoic, stiff, crank, looking like he was pretending to be relaxing. The woman, however, was intently watching us, glancing away occasionally, and then glancing back at us, with a most melancholy look on her face, every time the grill-smoke blew within sniffing range. She was restless, it seemed, perhaps feeling trapped. I thought that she would have liked some other people to talk to. But of course we did not know them, had no way to break the ice or establish a conversation on a windy day, and he seemed – perhaps it was my imagination – to be a bit of a snob.

Paul also noticed that the man's wife was watching us. She had that sort of look that my dog has when he knows that I have a biscuit but I am pretending that I don't have one and he is simply waiting as politely as he can manage for me to quit the inanity and give the damned thing over to him.

I raised my glass to toast. "To what?" Paul asked. "Nothing in particular" I replied. "Just hold it higher, so that it can be seen." He grasped my meaning immediately, and quaked with a rough, deep, sinister laugh. "Oh, Indeed!" he chuckled.

Now we lifted aloft big lumps of ripe Stilton, with an aroma redolent of a rotten sneaker, on our wide Bath Oliver crackers; now the slices of warm bread were slathered with soft butter, all enjoyed with visible gusto. Then it was time for the lamb, juice-spitting, tender chops taken off the grill at the perfect moment and cut away one by one from the rack, held in view and munched with pleasure, oozing juice down our chins as they melted in our mouths. Lamb-fat solidified in icicles as it dribbled down Paul's bushy beard.

Now she was really watching us; we pretended not to look her way, but I saw her lips move as she mouthed something; the wind would have drowned anything less than a shout; but what se said might have been a 'please, oh please'. Then I heard the husband berate her with a short, sharp, unintelligible, angry snap. The poor woman turned away from us and looked downcast. Her husband, who would not look our way, scowled.

"Nice boat, that, isn't it?" I commented to Paul.

"Why yes; Bloody dear one too, I'll wager" he replied.

"Must be comfortable," I added. "Probably has a sparkling galley."

"Oh certainly. All the modern conveniences. Doesn't seem like it gets much use, though."

"Cooking aboard can be a lot of trouble," I said.

"Amen to that," Paul replied.

We munched silently for a few moments, leaving, now, only a charnel-heap of cleaned rib bones on each plate. Several gulls, having seen from a distance what was going on in our cockpit, had settled in the water just astern of our boat, and were bobbing in the light green chop. They, too, were watching us, intently and expectantly.

"Top off your glass?" I asked, proffering the wine bottle.

"Oh, quite so, quite so, mate! Aye!"

"Boating is great, isn't it?"

"Quite so, oh yes, quite jolly, that!"

◆◆◆◆◆◆◆

97

Boat Dreams

When people speak of dreams coming true, the first thing that comes to mind, to the listener, is suddenness – a dream coming true manifested as a surprise, or sudden stroke of good fortune. But in reality, many dreams come true in the same way that a tree grows, or a wine matures; slowly, incrementally, in stages, more like plateaus, more like occasional pauses along the trail on an autumn hike up a New England mountainside. As one ascends the rocky-rubble path, first at the lowest elevations, and then later far higher, where the air becomes drier, cooler, and crisper; where the wind now begins to be felt; where the trees become straighter, thinner, and shorter, one still notices little but the boulders in the path; the sweat and exertion of climbing, gasping breath, the focused, intensive care of each footfall placed, so as not to stumble and fall.

Every once in a while the climber pauses, for a break in the effort, to take a swallow of water, to look around; and he or she immediately realizes the extent of the progress made since the last pause; it is greater than expected. These are truly serene moments, mentally and physically, despite the vibrant pulse in one's breast, and the decreasing urgency of breath; a sense of satisfaction comes from the realization of achievement; the summit is reachable, and will be attained. Thus the view of the end result changes, slightly; the mental image shifts, once again, and the urge returns stronger.

When the restoration of my old 33-foot wooden cabin cruiser *Fish Tales* was nearing completion, she stood on blocks and stands in my driveway, as high and dry as a boat could possibly be. I could only imagine what she would feel like cutting through the clearing blue waters off Point Judith; what her engines would sound like, and such. I was anxious to take this boat, the largest boat that I had ever owned, out into waters that I had never traversed, except perhaps on ferry boats to Block Island. In the late fall of the year before she was launched – and the odyssey of her restoration had now absorbed three years and more – I purchased a used LORAN-C receiver from a fellow in town who had advertised it in the local paper. I had wanted one, and they were not cheap, but his was offered for a reasonable price and was a good make and not very old. There were few GPS navigation systems in use among recreational boaters yet and LORAN was still in widespread use.

This receiver was made by Furuno and these were the days before the simplicity of chart plotters. The LORAN set, using a triangulation technique based on the time difference between signals received from land-based transmitting towers, displayed a set of coordinates that gave the navigator a precise position fix, displayed in either Latitude/Longitude coordinates, or LORAN "TD" (Time Differential) lines which were marked on charts in semicircular patterns. Most commercial fishermen used the TDs; the rest of us non-professionals used the Latitude/Longitude readout. Even then, it was up to the navigator to take these coordinates and plot them on a paper chart to establish a position fix; there was no such thing as an electronic chart or graphic display. Still, to me it was absolutely magical that this receiver could, at any given time, display my actual position in real time so that I could plot it, in clear weather or fog.

So on a few chill late autumn nights I stood at the steering console of *Fish Tales*, with the LORAN turned on, the manual open, learning how to use the thing, to zero it in properly and set it up right, pretending that I was out on the bay somewhere heading for Block Island or the Vineyard. Indeed, although the LORAN set would not work right with the boat out of water and not properly grounded, so the manual said, or because it was on land (unlike GPS, land masses interfered with LORAN reception – for it to work right you had to be out in open water), I still calculated the distance from where I was to an unseen goal, a waypoint, the 1BI green bell off the North Reef of Block Island. It was more than twenty-five miles, but I knew that, someday, most likely the following season, my boat and I would be there.

I remembered my first experience with LORAN as a young Coast Guardsman in 1975. Back then, LORAN "A" was in use, but it had limitations that I do not quite recall. LORAN "C" was more advanced and required an on-board computer of sorts but the results were more accurate. Our Coast Guard ship used both A and C but C only occasionally as it often malfunctioned. It also required a rather large module or unit and seemed clumsy, but this system demonstrated to me that in twenty years or so the technology had come a long way; the unit I purchased was the size of a small radio and gave highly accurate readouts on a backlit LCD screen. So I learned to use the unit, and played out my fantasies for the time being, navigating not an inch beyond my driveway, but I knew that I was getting there.

A couple of months later, a week before Christmas, the weather was unusually warm. It was a gusty, rainy night, and the Christmas lights in the trees and bushes throughout the neighborhood were jumping around in the restless wind squalls. We were hosting a a group of our friends over for a Christmas party and at one point it became so stuffy and warm in the house, and with everyone talking loudly and one of my tipsy friends couldn't be pried away from the piano, that I felt the sudden need to go outside for a few minutes for a breath of fresh air, alone. I took my drink with me, and stood out on the front lawn, in the hour before midnight, and felt the occasional raindrops whip by and watched *Fish Tales* in the driveway, bow pointed ever-westward, waiting patiently for spring, her 1950s-era flared bow and graceful old sedan cruiser lines looking as though they were ready to cut through the seas at any moment. Like many powerboats of her age, she sported a small decorative mast, resembling a swept-back cross, mounted on the deck just in front of the windshields. I had strung a couple of sets of colored Christmas lights on her little mast and had run an extension cord up there, and had even arranged a 12-volt connection to her topmost white Perko light globe and her big luminous Fresnel red and green sidelights, so that her navigational lights would be 'live'. She looked jolly with that little bit of Christmas holiday ornamentation and at that point I realized that indeed she would be launched, she would cruise, and that the long road of her restoration actually had a terminus, and that God willing, I would live to see it and have many adventures aboard her. It was a precious moment, and it caused me to forget the rain and the party noise inside and focus on a dream that was gradually inching closer to eventual reality.

◆◆◆◆◆◆◆

Hurricane at the Dinghy Dock

The Dinghy Dock bar was crowded with marooned charter customers and almost everyone was drunk, even though it was barely mid-afternoon. There were a lot of folks there from different countries. I remember the two bearded young German guys and their aging dad. It was his 65th birthday, and the night before they had arranged a surprise present for him – they sent a local prostitute to his hotel room. While he was thus occupied, they stayed at the bar late into the evening while the first warm unsettled gusts from Hurricane Lenny offshore began to rustle the coconut palms. One of the sons finished off a beer and commented how cool it would be if only a big U-boat from the days of the Reich would surface in the middle of Oyster Pond. Everyone was feeling just a little bit trapped, after all.

Ryan's Dinghy Dock, on the edge of Oyster Pond, the only real hurricane hole in St. Martin, was a quaint little bar run by a hippie American expatriate. It was close to the actual dinghy dock, which was generally a busy place because most to St. Martin's charter fleet operates out of Oyster Pond. But now there was a freak late-season hurricane coming, so the charters were cancelled, charter customers and tourists were stranded, it was all a mess – broken plans and thwarted vacation dreams under gray, wet, suffocatingly hot and humid skies. Hurricane Lenny was coming, moving weirdly from west to east in mid-November, and he was taking his time. Waiting was the tough part; the storm was moving very slowly, but now it was very close, and all the flights out of Juliana airport had been cancelled.

So everyone was drunk now simply because there was nothing else to do. Ryan kept a tab tally on a yellow legal pad of what everyone owed. He would be paid, he knew, sooner or later. There was a hurricane coming and there was absolutely nothing for anyone to do but sit around and wait for it. Everyone knew that it was going to be bad, and that made the waiting worse, so people drank, and kept on drinking.

When morning broke on the day that the hurricane was expected to hit, I awoke knowing that there was no way that I could spend another moment in that hotel room waiting for it under a leaden sky. The catamaran that we had sailed to St. Martin was secured with a spider-web of lines out at the end of its slip, away from the dock to accommodate anticipated line stretch, so there was no going aboard, and besides I had taken all of my gear off the boat anyway. Hilarious laughter from the waterfront bar, carried on the wind gusts, greeted me as I descended the steep hill from the hotel, alternately louder, then softer or inaudible. It only made me want to get there faster, afraid that I was missing something, a good joke, or the last bottle of Carib beer.

The wind had freshened, arriving in ever more frequent squalls. St. Martin had seemed a happy, colorful, tropical paradise when I had arrived a couple of days earlier, but now there was a pre-storm tension in the air as low, scudding, dirty-gray clouds raced across the island, and the rain showers began to lash the landscape with greater frequency, blowing, slanted, soaking at times. Everything was warm, humid, and wet; clothes damp, shoes squishy. The wind whipped the coconut palm fronds around cruelly, tearing them off, fragments of palm littering the road and the stubbly Bermuda grass on what passed for little lawns. The wind was not yet strong enough to be dangerous; nothing of any size was flying about. That would come in a few hours. Down by the Pond, workers were closing the shutters to protect windows, and the awnings along the waterfront were bellying and flapping; they would soon tear if not taken in. Young men employed by the charter companies were zooming about the pond in gray Italian inflatables, making final adjustments to anchors and lines. The chop was kicking up even in the pond now, making it wet work for them.

A big crowd had gathered at the bar, all the familiar faces from the last few days. They had it tough; they were Americans and Europeans mostly, who had paid big money to charter yachts but were now marooned ashore, their charters canceled, their deposits forfeited. Those were the rules, read the fine print. No refunds for hurricanes, but then again no one actually believed that there would be one this late in the season. So they stood around, resigned to their situation, annoyed that they were not going to get their money back just the same. As the wind rose, and the humming sound of the wind in wire rigging jumped an octave, we all stood around and guzzled beer, talking, laughing, and joking while Ryan in his Hawaiian shirt, long hair and bushy moustache kept the cold clear bottles of Carib beer moving and clinking. What had been a tropical paradise a day before, with hot intense sun under sapphire blue skies, green palm trees, sea breezes, and exotica such as Captain Oliver's multicolored macaw, had now turned upside-down.

But for all that, we had the Dinghy Dock, a place unique in all the world, and its jolly, skinny, lovable ageing hippie proprietor whose main goal at the moment was to raise enough money by working and then selling the business to move to the southern part of Thailand which, supposedly, had become the new chic spot for expatriate American flower children who still believed in warm climates, free love, cheap living, plentiful ganja, and the Path of Enlightenment. But for now, we had him at the Dinghy Dock, tall, gangly, friendly, hairy, knob-kneed and knob-elbowed, tanned and gap-toothed, large square-ish glasses, and extremely sociable. Ryan was our friend, provider, and protector, laid-back embodiment of coolness, friendliness, and understanding. He knew how we felt. He had been through hurricanes before, and when he heard that this one was coming, he stowed extra cases of beer, whisky, and everything else that he knew would be needed.

Hurricane Lenny was a slow-moving hurricane. It did not slam into St. Martin, but took its time, crept up on the island, wound up its punch, and then started hammering. By noon, a sizable crowd had gathered at the Dinghy Dock, and the rain was coming down in sheets, wind-driven, as the outer fringes of the hurricane approached. The wind came in squalls that corresponded to the cyclonic bands of the storm; squall, then moderation; alternating, with the squalls, hour by hour, becoming more intense in wind velocity. Things were beginning to blow around, such as the brown shards of bark from the palm trees, and some broken fronds. The air was very warm, very tropical and humid; nothing anywhere would dry. Dampness permeated everything, rain and dripping wetness and stifling heat. Perspiration did not evaporate; it simply joined the moisture from the windblown rain and ran down our foreheads and bodies in little rivulets.

At the bar, though, the pony bottles of Carib beer were cold and tasty and condensation beaded all over the outside of the bottles making them not only slippery but visually appealing, and each bottle was served with a little wedge of lime stuck in the mouth, just like a Corona. In fact, Carib beer tastes a lot like Corona. We had Carib beer and of course plenty of Mount Gay rum – it is the dominant brand down there and there is plenty of rum in the islands and it is quite cheap – but also green bottles of the Mexican beer President.

I had gone riding around the island with my friend Stan in a rented jeep and we went to an out-of-the-way beach at the end of a long dirt road where there was a bar and cabana. It was owned by a big African fellow who was truly African, not brown at all but extremely black so that his skin had a sheen like blued gun metal. His face broke into a broad grin when I asked for a cold President and then gripped it in my hand. He pointed to my hand and laughed, a big deep, jolly laugh, and said "Ha, ha, you see, that is what we call shaking hands with the President! Hey, you want to shake hands with the President?" I had to laugh too.

A hired cook was grilling burgers outside and Stan and I bought a couple and sat at a table right down next to the beach where we could view the panorama of the water and eat our burger and beer lunch. Then we noticed that most of the women on the beach were topless and some were entirely naked. So Stan looked at me and said, "Now I know why we wear dark sunglasses." We seemed to be looking out at the horizon.

But as we sat there, I began to understand – and this came to me like an epiphany, like a big rogue sea breaking over a ship and washing the decks - that there is in fact a dual purpose to clothing; the first and most familiar is to cover one's body parts, to spare the exposure of one's private areas to the view of others. But now I saw that it serves another purpose – to protect the inadvertent passer-by from having to view the less choice cuts, if you will, of others when unclothed. Few bodies on a nude beach, I learned, look better without the covering of a bathing suit; in fact for some, I would venture that the shame of nakedness is not so much in being naked, but in having one's nakedness dearly offend the aesthetic sensibilities of someone else.

Now we were back at the Dinghy Dock and a diminutive but sturdy young woman, Kelly, was talking about airplanes. She was in her mid-thirties and was an airline pilot, flying big jets like Boeing's 767s. She and her boyfriend had been on a charter and were now stuck like everyone else. She was very intelligent and serious and professional in her demeanor and did not seem the type of person who cared much for laughter or frivolity; in fact she seemed a bit severe. There had been an air disaster recently some-where off the east coast of the United States; a jumbo jet had plunged into the Atlantic from a considerable altitude, with total loss of life; a fisherman in the vicinity had heard a sonic boom, or so he thought, and we were discussing whether or not it was feasible for a big jet in an uncontrolled dive to break the sound barrier before impact. "Not really" she replied, downing another shot of Sambuca and smoking a cigarette. "The fuselage would begin twisting and contorting; it would rip apart. They are not designed to break the sound barrier, it would never do so intact." This was the sort of cheerful talk we had in the afternoon as the hurricane approached and started shredding the canvas awnings of the closed shops along the wharf.

The back room of the Dinghy Dock was simply a room with tables, sliding glass doors that opened onto the dock, and bookshelves – walls of bookshelves, loaded with dog-eared, well-thumbed paperbacks mostly in English but in other languages, many sans covers, that had been donated to Ryan's Dinghy Dock Lending Library. The rules were simple; borrow what you like, just return it when you're done – or substitute something else – and all donations are appreciated even if not tax-deductible. So the library had grown to include every kind of genre and topic under the sun arranged in absolutely no particular order or classification. But that's what made it wonderful, the element of surprise. In the days ahead, this little library would alleviate the boredom of many a hurricane castaway.

Late in the afternoon the wind became so strong that it was becoming dangerous. A wooden shingle blew off a building and hit a fellow who was walking down the road in the cheek and opened his face. While a couple of people struggled to get over the roads to get him to a doctor, Stan and I headed up the hill to the Columbus Hotel where our skipper, Walter, had arranged for a room for us. Walter was the owner of the big catamaran Cressida, that Stan, the hired delivery skipper, and I as hired crew had brought down to St. Martin from New York a few days before.

When I finally awoke, the morning after the hurricane hit St. Martin, it was nearly noon. The terrible wind had finally eased some time during the wee hours of the morning, and I had been able to stumble stiffly out of the bathroom and back into the bedroom proper and collapse onto the big king-sized bed. The wind was abating and I was no longer afraid that it would burst the sliding glass patio doors into the room and kill us with flying glass. That's why Stan and I had been hiding in the cramped bathroom, sitting on the counter, in case the big glass doors exploded into the room. We would be decapitated, or worse, I thought, because there was no place else in the room where one could hide or be protected.

Stan, a seasoned sailor, had been hired by the boat's owner, Wally, to help sail the boat to the island, where Wally had planned to lease it to a charter fleet home ported in Oyster Pond. It had been a difficult, stormy passage, and when we finally reached St. Martin we learned that a late-season hurricane had developed and was headed toward the island. Stan and I had spent the night of the storm in a little hotel up the street from the Oyster Pond docks. The skipper had arranged a room for us, since it was not possible to remain on the boat. Wally was staying somewhere else – we didn't know where – with acquaintances, at a private home with plenty of food and comforts. We had been left to shift for ourselves which was, in our opinion, still much better than being stuck in the same place with Wally, whom, we discovered early in the voyage, was a weird, obnoxious crank.

As I gradually came to my senses on the damp bed, a gray light filtered into the hotel room. The air was hot and humid and there was no electricity and no running water. I opened the drapes and looked out upon the scene of devastation under overcast skies. The patio outside was a mess - parts of the roof had blown off and there were smashed, splintered timbers and roof tiles scattered every- where. It was still windy, but the hurricane had passed.

There was no coffee and no hope for any. Stan awoke in the easy chair about the same time, and we both stepped out onto the patio, rubbing our eyes, still groggy from the nearly sleepless night, trying to take it all in. I had a small bottle of water – tepid but fresh – and poured most of it into a cup, filling it two-thirds, and the rest with Mount Gay rum from a half-full bottle that I had brought up from the Dinghy Dock bar down the street the night before. I took a big swallow and handed it to Stan. Instead of recoiling from the liquor, as he usually did, he took it happily, and took a long pull at it, even though it was warm. Any other time he might have gagged.

"I'm going up the hill to have a look around" I said, slinging my camera and a small knapsack with a water bottle and the Mount Gay. "Want to come along?"

"I'll stay here in case Wally comes back" he said, "He might bring some food."

"F..., Wally," I said. "He won't bring us dogshit."

"Fine then. Let's go and see what we can find for ourselves."

106

There was a path across the street from the hotel that led up a scrubby hill to a promontory with an overlook that provided a good view of everything around, including Oyster Pond. An ancient naval cannon was mounted on a stone base resembling a carriage at the top of the hill, pointing out to sea. The hurricane had not budged it, but the odd cacti, grasses, and shrubs that covered the hill had been strangely altered. Any part of a cactus – and these were sizable, tough cacti – above a point horizontally level with the top of the hill had been sheared cleanly off, as though a great scythe from the sea had swept across the top of the hill and had cut away anything not protected in its shadow, on a direct horizontal plane. It was eerie. Even from the hilltop, we could hear the roar of the breakers on the beaches below. White, angry surf and big swells were still rolling ashore on the unprotected beaches, while occasional drizzle and mist blew by. Down in Oyster Pond, we could see the crazed jumble of masts along the ring of the pond of all the sailboats that had blown ashore and now lay on their sides on the beach, at odd senseless angles to one another, stranded and damaged. "This island is one hell of a mess," I said. "Let's go back and have another drink and a smoke."

Back at the hotel, Stan and I moved a big piece of broken roof – part of an eave – out of the way, dragging it off the patio so that it would not be stepped on by bare feet or tripped over. It was a mess of splinters, nails, and jagged wood. As we did so, a door to a room on the second-floor opened, and a heavy-set older man stepped out onto the balcony. He was dressed casually in a Hawaiian shirt and shorts and spoke with a British accent. He and his wife had been staying there for some time, and had apparently come through the storm all right. She was still asleep, he said.

"Do you fellows have any bottled water?" he asked.

"Not really," I replied. "I filled our wastebaskets and every pot and pan we could find from the taps before the storm hit, so we have some clean water, if you need it."

"Oh, no. I mean for you fellows. Here." He reached down and handed us four liter-bottles of French bottled water. "Take care, conserve it. Trust me, chaps; you'll be needing it later on."

"Come have a drink with us," I offered.

"No, thank you mates, we're all set here. I have to tend to the missus. Be careful and take care. Cheers." With that, he went back into the room and shut the door.

"Decent fellow," I said to Stan, who nodded in agreement.

While we had been exploring the hilltop, a French couple had pulled up a couple of chairs and a table on the patio and when we returned they were still seated there, drinking a big bottle of wine. They spoke no English, but the tall, long black-haired woman that was the wife or girlfriend – they seemed young – was laughing and talking loudly and animatedly and was apparently quite drunk. At least she seems happy, I thought to myself.

I looked down into the hotel's inground pool. The chlorinated water was still clean and clear, but the blue bottom of the pool was a crazy-quilt of black asphalt roof tile squares. There were some palm fronds and a couple of small green coconuts floating in it. The sun had begun to burn through and it was getting hot. "I'm going in" I said to Stan. "Sounds good to me too" he replied.

We stripped down to our shorts – after all there was a lady nearby – and went into the pool, removing the palm fronds and floating junk. The cool water felt good.

While we were thus splashing around, I suddenly noticed that the woman had stood up, and, despite the emphatic entreaties of her male companion, had stripped off her bathing suit, every stitch. Stan noticed too; then I saw his jaw drop as she hopped across the patio laughing and saying something very fast and very loud in French, and then swan-dove into the pool directly behind Stan.

A very loud and earnest exchange ensued between the laughing girl and her male companion, who was quite upset with her, probably because there were two other strange men in the same pool with her and she was completely naked. She was finally persuaded to climb out and put her bathing suit back on; Stan and I were mum, of course, and did our best to pretend that nothing was happening, Stan keeping his back to her while she was in the pool. Finally they stood up and took what was left of the bottle and made their way around the corner to a different hotel, presumably the one that they were staying at.

"She had very nice, long black hair," Stan said.

"Yes, she certainly did, didn't she?"

A while later, we went down to the Dinghy Dock Bar looking for something to eat, and were happy to see that much of the debris around the docks had been cleaned up, or at least pushed aside, and we saw, to our delight, that the Dinghy Dock was, remarkably, unshuttered and open. It had suffered no real damage, and there was

Ryan, its proprietor, the American hippie expatriate, behind the bar, operating some type of propane-powered portable stove linked to a big rusty gas bottle set on the ground. Stan and I had sauntered down to the dock – it was around eleven in the morning now – not expecting to find anything open; there were boat owners out on the docks, trying to assess damage to their boats, and salvaging clothing and other soaked items from down below.

It was still a little breezy and overcast and an occasional rain shower spattered the docks. I could smell coffee brewing; the aroma was heavenly. The little bar was nearly full; people were drinking coffee, rum, coffee with rum, beer, every variety of beverage, mostly with alcohol. Ryan had put out open cartons of Parmalat milk on the bar so that folks could lighten their coffee. There was sugar in little damp packets. Ryan was busy, hopping around, and in response to a query from a fellow at the bar about running out of things, he shook his head and smiled,

"Oh, no! I've been through this hurricane thing a few times. I know how to plan ahead." Indeed, in the few days prior to the hurricane, when it was becoming near-certain that the island would be in its path, Ryan ordered extra cases of beer and liquor, eggs, bread, batteries, bottled water, propane, ice…as much as he could cram into the limited storage space that the Dinghy Dock building afforded. Now it would pay off. There was no food around, only at the Dock. Ryan had multiple pans going. He was making breakfast sandwiches for everyone. There was no electricity, so eggs were scrambled in a pan over the gas grill. There was cheese, there was bacon, and the bread was toasted, sometimes blackened a little, over the blue flames. It was grilled bread; a little crude, perhaps – like camping and toasting your bread over a fire – but it worked, and everyone ate.

Thereafter, ever day, in addition to breakfast, Ryan, who was a rather decent cook, made one main dish – and lots of it – for the rest of the day, lunch and dinner. These meals were planned, their ingredients ordered in advance, and it changed every day, although there was nothing else on the menu. But there was no need. Each meal was a one-pot type, spaghetti and meatballs, or chicken a la king, chicken curry, or a big stew, something that involved a main dish over rice or noodles. It was good, satisfying, and filling; the portions were generous and nobody starved. Ryan kept a log on a notepad of who ate and drank what, and everyone was expected to settle up before leaving the island – whenever that might be. If you wanted to sit at the bar and drink rum, you were given the bottle, a glass, and a little notepad and pencil to keep track of your own tally. You mixed your own drinks, poured them yourself – weak or killer, the choice was up to the drinker. So, depending on what sort of a day you were having, you self-medicated accordingly.

It went on like this for several days until we were finally able to get off the island on the first departing flight out of damaged Juliana Airport. Because the runway had been damaged, flights had to take off with minimal fuel, so we stopped in San Juan to fill the tanks before going on to Newark, N.J., not the last stop by far in what would be my long journey home to New-England. As we flew through the night, I looked out my window into the cold moonlit blackness at the sea below, the hundreds of leagues that we had taken many days to sail over, crossing our path, and now crossing that gulf in mere hours at more than five hundred knots and more than five miles up in the sky. I felt my tired body relax, settle, conform to the seat like a wad of silly-putty, and at long last fell into a brief, but deep, sleep.

◆◆◆◆◆◆◆

Late Fall Ferry Run

The last time I took the slow ferry to Block Island, it was a late autumn afternoon, departing the dock an hour before sunset. It was a spur of the moment decision; a lark, a need to go out on the sea, even if just for a little while; completely impulsive. The sea was steely gray and calm as the big ferry plowed monotonously through it, plodding toward the island. It was the last week of October, the usual time for unquiet water, but the sea had no anger in it today; that moment had passed two days earlier when a gale sprang up out of the southeast, and then had blown itself out.

I knew that the weather could change fast and mercilessly at this time of year, but that was not a concern for this day. Daylight was waning; high clouds had moved in from the east, like a pall across the sky, but blue sky was still visible to the westward, beyond the encroaching blanket of clouds. It was just after sunset, and I had watched the fiery orange orb of the sun sink out of sight behind the dark mass of the island as the ferry pushed onward toward the harbor, whose twinkling lights had begun to appear against the darkling mass of the land.

A soft mist seemed to have risen from the sea, a slight haze or cold fog, barely discernible, all around the island, giving the distant harbor and waterfront an ethereal, blue-and-soot, darkened, Old World look. I stood on the uppermost, exposed deck, feeling how the days were turning cold. The ferry had few passengers on this late-day run, and there were no passengers on the open deck other than myself and an anonymous person in a parka with its hood drawn tightly, sitting motionless at the far end of the deck, unspeaking, remarkably alone. I could not be sure whether the person was a man or a woman; nor did I much care to discover, despite the usual natural curiosity inherent in every person to know all obvious things, at least, about another when only two people are on the deck of a steamer with naught but water surrounding. One usually senses intuitively when the other wishes to be left alone; thus, I did not disturb.

The ferry pressed along like the cold metal bulk that it was; ponderously, without the sweet sea-kindly motion that one would wish to feel under one's feet, like the motion of a yacht, or sailing-ship in harmony with the forces around it. I caught a whiff of diesel exhaust, biting, pungent, fake-sweet but non-nourishing. It was decidedly unlike the incense-like wafting tart scent of a hardwood fire in a brick hearth hanging in the air on a crisp winter's night; still, the familiar diesel stink reminded me of years gone by, of days and months serving on a small naval ship at sea in my youth, a youth long gone and misspent. I recalled how the pervasive flavor of diesel fuel permeated the entire ship, ultimately; even the loaves of bread in the galley, for it seems to me that bread has an affinity for raw diesel fuel and will absorb the off-flavor of it from the air no matter how tightly the bread is wrapped. After a month aboard ship I became used to the taste, such that after awhile I no longer noticed it, and might have considered it insignificant, forgetting my initial disgust. Only after a time ashore, eating fresh bread, did I discover, upon returning to the ship, how much diesel smell the bread actually did absorb. While the flavor was once again initially repugnant, I quickly became accustomed to the fuel-flavor in the bread all over again, as before; but I never preferred it.

I walked stiff-kneed down the iron stairway and pulled open the heavy door to the passenger deck cabin. The aroma of steamed hot dogs and hot coffee borne on a blast of warm, humid, engine-oily air greeted me; a cup of bilge-water coffee, more restorative for its heat than its content, seemed attractive. It will do more good, I thought, than those bloated, pale pink, limp, grease-sweating hot dogs rolling eternally on the steel rods of the hot dog grilling machine.

I returned to the open deck, to find myself truly alone; the parka-wrapped mystery person was gone. We docked; I looked over the rain and saw the shoreline, littered with the brown, torn and dying sea-vegetation that had been cast up by the storm two days before. Once the cars were gone and most of the people had left the ferry, I descended the last stairway and found myself ashore, like the seaweed, tossed up on the brown strand, cast up with nowhere to go.

◆◆◆◆◆◆◆

Express Delivery

I begin by briefly saying that I have known a lot of fellows who can handle a motorboat, but there's no one quite like Captain Bill. Cap'n Bill can move a twin-screw boat an inch or so at a time – I'm not kidding – no matter what the prevailing wind and current are doing. He can bring a 30-ft heavy sport fisherman up against a fuel dock, walking it sideways like a swimming crab, only even more gracefully than a crab, and lay it up against the piling so gently that if the rub-rail had been lined with fresh eggs, none would break, you'd go without your omelet. This may seem an exaggeration but I swear it's not.

I had been invited by Captain Bill to serve as Mate on board a powerboat delivery from Rhode Island to Ocean City, Maryland. I was excited by the prospect of taking a relatively fast boat on a delivery trip, rather than a slow sailboat, which had been the type of delivery I was used to doing myself. The Captain, a seasoned skipper, wrinkled his nose and remarked gruffly "I don't do blow boats anymore. Not unless it's really something special."

The trip ahead was, roughly, 340 nautical miles. The Cap'n planned to do it in two days, stopping the first night; I had expected him to take the boat on the outside and run nonstop the projected 20 hours. I learned, once we got going that this was not possible since the boat would require refueling well before that!

Our boat was a relatively late model 30' Luhrs sport fisherman, with twin turbocharged Yanmar diesels. A 30-footer is not considered a large sport fisherman by any standard; in fact it is considered a borderline 'pocket' sport fisherman. Still, it had a tuna tower, outriggers, and looked the part. It was in fine condition, overall, and a couple of days before departure, we brought her over to the fuel dock and pumped 300 gallons of diesel into her, topping off her tank. This would get us as far as Sandy Hook, New Jersey, with little to spare, which surprised me a little, since I would have expected better mileage out of a boat that size, and diesel-powered at that.

Before we set out, however, we noted one problem – a leak in the pressurized water line under the galley sink. We weren't equipped to repair it, so there would be no pressurized fresh water during the trip and thus no on-board showers. We would drink bottled water and have to wait to shower when we reached our destination.

For food, we had each brought sandwiches, crackers, snack bars, and such. "Don't worry," Cap'n Bill said. "We'll have the chance to eat civilized."

I didn't mind the idea of being a 'stink-pot' sailor for a couple of days, not one bit, in fact I welcomed the change, and in fact my first big boat years ago had been a power boat. It had been a vintage 1952 twin-screw, 33-foot wooden Richardson sedan cruiser. It usually ran at eight knots, because if I had pushed her any faster something might, and usually did, break. She was gasoline-fueled, and her original flathead Chrysler Crown engines and Zenith carburetors had been designed back in the days when gasoline prices had been something on the order of 10 cents a gallon, so it was in the best interests of my wallet to push her round bilge along at no greater than hull speed. There were no trim tabs, and although she was capable of real speed in short bursts, I rarely ever ran her hard. Now, under way, I was learning a few things about trying to average 20 knots in choppy seas, and it decidedly did not feel much like sailing.

The first thing I noted, from a purely fluid-dynamics perspective, is that no matter how fast you are going, swells, waves, or seas don't care. In fact, they pay no attention to you or your comfort at all, they just move along on their merry way, and it's usually a lot slower than you want to travel, and almost never in a direction, size, or interval that will help you go faster, or more comfortably along, not one little bit. You will pound, slam, plow, skew, lurch, yaw, plop, thunk, bounce, and flounce along with bone-jarring constancy, and the faster you try to go, the more it will hurt. Your stomach and internal organs will never be still, and will be constantly trying to escape the confines of your body, through either of the body's two main exits, north, or worse, south. It's very important that the powerboater, Cap'n or Mate, keep those innards contained.

Although I am not a medical student, I also nonetheless acquired on this trip a real appreciation for the wonderful way that the human body, although flexible, is still held firmly together with cartilage and connective tissue; otherwise mine would, I am sure, have flown apart quite early in the trip and the boat would be followed, for some time, by a flock of feeding gulls much like a herring trawl. I therefore realized, after about an hour, that I did not need to hold onto various valued parts of my body in order to retain them; besides, I did not have enough arms and hands for that.

Forget the old expression "One hand for yourself, the other for the ship." No, it's "Both hands for yourself" because the Captain is driving the ship.'

You really can't do much – eat, or read, or drink except from a water bottle on occasion. Hearing protectors are a must to prevent your gray matter from turning to jelly from the high-decibel whine of the turbos, so there's no talking, and the only sign language the Cap'n and I know is the Rhode Island Driver's Salute, and we were not yet at a point in the voyage where we were in any disagreement such that we might be of a mind to exchange it.

So you're basically in a bouncing cocoon, with most sensory input disabled except for your sight. "This ain't fast," Cap'n Bill growls. "Not really. I took a squadron of boats down the coast once on a multiple delivery, mix of gas and diesel boats. The gas boats were faster than the diesels. Hell, they could pass anything on the water – 'cept the FUEL DOCK!" he roared and then chuckled.

Attempts to drink the first – and only – coffee of the day were equally frustrating. This was especially true on the second morning, when Cap'n Bill was in a hurry to get going early and we rounded Sandy Hook in choppy seas going at an ambitious clip because he wanted to make time. I had brewed some coffee and had a hand-warming tin cup full of it when we hit the first seas going around the point. What followed was a half-hour – as the coffee cooled – of holding the cup with both hands and working it up and down, as though I were perpetually making an offering to the Sea Gods, or throwing rice at the bride at a wedding, a ridiculous movement I am sure, but it kept the coffee from spilling, yet at the same time I could not get it near enough to my lips long enough to steal a sip. No, Murphy's Law states that as soon as you get it close enough to your face to get a sip, it will rise up, drench, and scald your face. I knew this, since I am quite familiar with Murphy's Laws. What actually happened was that as soon as the coffee was cool enough to drink, we hit an especially big sea and it went all over me, the console, and the cockpit floor, thus becoming, as it must have been intended, an offering to the Sea Gods via the scuppers. I was so busy with my own coffee that I never noticed what Cap'n Bill did with his.

I recognized, from the start, that I was the junior guy aboard, and I was fine with that. Cap'n Bill doesn't waste words, and is not taken to a lot of silliness or smiles. His humor is dry, but genuine, and if you ask him a direct question, and you'll get a straight answer, all the time. That's easy, because you always know where you stand with the Cap'n, and if you mess up, well, you'll know right away too.

We left Narragansett Bay on a wet, windy, rain-soaked morning, rounded rough 'P'int Judy' and headed toward Long Island Sound. Cap'n Bill is a clever, strategic guy; we went inside Fisher's Island, then down the Sound, hugging the inside coast of Long Island to protect us against the southerly swell and give us docile enough seas so that we could keep up a good pace. We passed through New York, under the many neat bridges, and into busy, hot, murky, cloudy New York Harbor, past Lady Liberty, under the big Verrazzano Narrows Bridge, and off toward Sandy Hook to refuel. Thunderheads were building; it was hot and sultry at the fuel dock when we finally arrived in Sandy Hook's Atlantic Highlands shore; skinny kids were crabbing with long-handled dip nets. I glanced longingly at the shore, but realized that I would be spending a sweaty, smelly night on an anchor out in the bay, probably with lightning flashing all around. Surely the anchor would hold if set right. Oh well, I told myself, that's sailing, er, boating.

Ah, but no, not with this Cap'n! "We need a slip for the night" he told the dock attendant, pulling out the owner's charge card and paperwork. My heart leaped; images of a bar of soap and a glass of beer filled my mind's eye, in quick succession. Yes, there was one slip available! We tied up, plugged in the power cord, and Cap'n Bill turned on the cabin A/C. In my bubbly joy, I told Cap'n Bill that, if he should repair ashore, I would be pleased to buy him a beer; he pulled at a corner of his shirt, looked up and said "Fine, right after I get out of this stink suit!"

The Atlantic Highlands marina was huge compared to what I was used to. There were perhaps a couple thousand boats nestled behind a breakwater, and the place had showers, a tackle shop, restaurant, and pub. I made it to the restaurant in a jiffy after a good scrubbing, and soon Cap'n Bill wandered over as well, similarly refreshed, and we had the chance to 'eat civilized' as he had promised, and relax on the upper deck where someone pointed out a pod of dolphins frolicking in the oily-looking, orange-reflecting shallows at sunset.

After Cap'n Bill had retired to his bunk I returned to the upper deck of the restaurant and sat watching, with calm, relaxed

116

detachment, the distant lights of New York Bay, Raritan Bay, and the Narrows Bridge for awhile. The many buoys out in the bay were blinking red and green and I saw the lights of various small vessels moving back and forth in various directions, and I thought how indeed I do love this.

Whenever I feel that way, in quiet contemplation, I think about my old, weathered copy of Chapman's Piloting that I bought way back in 1974, because an older boat-owner friend had told me that it was the 'boater's bible' and that I must absolutely have one. The book's long-time founder and editor, Charles F. Chapman, was 93 at the time, and in his preface to that 51st edition, he closed with "Could the author live over again those glorious 60 boating years, without change, he would be happy..." I have always felt bad for Captain Chapman, over the years, after reading that seemingly sad note, because he knew innately that his time on the sea was just about done. Yet people who truly love boating and the sea would do it for a thousand years or more, and never cease, if they could. I remind myself every year that I must make more of an effort to get out on the water at each and every opportunity, because someday I, too, will feel just like old Chap did, and so many others like us have as well.

It was fortunate that Cap'n Bill chose to take a slip that night, for during the middle of the night, an awful thunderstorm broke overhead, with frequent lightning flashes visible through the translucent foredeck hatch, torrential rains the likes of which Noah saw, and a single, initial gust of wind so powerful that it forced the boat up hard against the pilings.

In the early morning we were once again on our way, down the long and interesting New Jersey coast, past Manasquan, past Barnegat light, past Atlantic City's high-rises and eventually Cape May. As we crossed Delaware Bay, threatening clouds built up once again, and a black squall surrounded us off the Delaware coast. I was anxious, but oddly, I never saw a hint of concern on the Cap'n's face the entire trip. "Well, we may have to dodge a few thunder-boomers here and there" was all he said. In the end, there was little lightning, not much wind, but torrents of rain that happily made the sea lie down so that we could maintain our speed. Eventually the high-rise buildings of Ocean City, Md., materialized through the clouds and mist, and we passed through the inlet and were in a slip at our final destination by five o'clock in the evening.

Clearly, we were in sport fishing heaven; boats looking just like ours, feature for feature, only larger – lined up like soldiers in full dress at attention, their outriggers in line like shouldered arms with bayonets, ready for parade or inspection. "Fish-killin's big here," Cap'n Bill said, matter-of-factly.

Although it was hot and humid, I could relax, now; the trip was over. In the morning, we would go to the airport to get the rental car and take turns driving home. In the meantime, this marina had all the right stuff, showers and bathrooms, a tackle shop with hot coffee early in the morning, a nice outdoor bar and a restaurant, even better overall than the marina in Sandy Hook. Owners and captains sat around the bar and talked about bringing in white marlin that day, caught in the Gulf Stream forty and more miles out. I almost expected to see Papa Hemingway with a tall daiquiri in front of him, drunkenly regaling the other fishermen with his own whoppers. Instead, here was Cap'n Bill, buying us both a drink and a truly civilized dinner. "I'll bet you're feeling muscles you never knew you had" he grinned. "We certainly got beat up a little bit, but that's to be expected on an express delivery. But you'll sleep well tonight!" he said, and I agreed.

It had been a bumpy trip, but there were times when the sea was relatively docile, and it was occasionally my turn to take the helm for awhile. The last stretch had been from Little Egg inlet, above Atlantic City, down past Cape May and into Delaware Bay, nearly sixty miles. I stood at the helm rather than sitting, since I was used to that as a sailboat skipper, and when the seas allowed, extended the trim tabs all the way, pushing the bow down, and then throttled up, zooming planar across the seas for almost three hours in a ride that was nothing less than exhilarating. But I had a sore body now, and I also realized that if I were making the same trip in a sailboat, it would take nearly a week unless I had a crew of at least three and we sailed on the outside 24/7. I might do that someday, too, I thought. But for the moment, I was content; the rich green eelgrass of the salt marsh surrounding the marina looked a lot like crab country; heck it even smelled like blueshells. I looked at the restaurant menu; fried softshell crabs. Oh, my.

"Dinner's on me tonight, that's the custom," Cap'n said. "Know what you want?"

"I Sure do!"

♦♦♦♦♦♦♦

A New Captain's First Charter

I was a newly minted Captain, and was faced with my first weekend sailing charter. This was what I had always dreamed of doing, I reminded myself, so why was I so nervous?

It wasn't as though I were new to boats and boating. I have spent my life in boats, growing up in Rhode Island, on Narragansett Bay. I served as a seaman on a ship in the Coast Guard as a young man, cruising down in the Gulf of Mexico, and have owned and sailed a number of boats since childhood, ranging in size from a canoe to a twin-screw cabin cruiser to a 45-foot cruising yacht. But I had never, in all those years, taken the time to become an officially licensed captain, except for once when, fresh out of the service, I had obtained a 'six-pack' limited license to operate our Yacht Club's harbor launch. But that was more than thirty years earlier. Now, at age 53, I was standing on a pier in Newport, R.I., on a warm October morning, waiting for three business gentlemen from Massachusetts. They would be my charges for a weekend's paid charter on a 40-foot sailboat, and I was a mite jittery. It was my first real assignment as a hired captain, after all, with people aboard, not a simple boat delivery. Stress, and pressure, like nasty little devils, had bound me hand and foot, stretched me upon a rack, and were gleefully cranking it tighter one notch at a time. The more uneasy I felt, the faster they cranked. I could almost hear the pawls clicking.

Later, when I described this uncomfortable sensation to my friend Captain Tom, a long-time all-around skipper and tugboat captain, he laughed a hearty, but well-meaning laugh, and roared, "Oh, I know! I know the feeling! And the worst part is you can't show it, can't look anywhere for sympathy! You have to step aboard like it's the thousandth time you've done it, act like you know everything, calm, confident, in charge. You can't screw up, not one little bit, or seem to be unfamiliar with anything! They're watching you, and at the slightest sign of weakness or uncertainty, they will get scared, especially if they're not sailors themselves! You don't want that to happen."

In the dark winter of the early months of 2009, business was scarce, and I had little to do. I felt that my world and all that I had accomplished or built in my marketing business over the years had been all for naught. I felt, as Joshua Slocum had written, "cast up from the old sea, so to speak," but in my case the sea was the sea of life. One frozen February evening, at our local Irish pub, while talking to Captain Tom over a pint of Guinness and despairing over my poor fortunes, I listened to him talk about how busy he was running tugboats down in New York harbor, and in my envy, I suddenly had an idea, like a flash-bulb going off in my head: I resolved that I should go back to sea. He enthusiastically approved of this idea, and told me I should do so, that the change of life would do me good, would probably help me provide better for my family, get me out from behind a desk, and generally be a good move. "With all the sea time you have, you should easily qualify for a license," he said. Captain Tom is a few years older than me, but not many, and since I have never believed that one is ever too old to change course, I thought, why not give it a try. My wife expressed doubts; "Your business will return when the economy begins to come around again," she said. "When it does, you will never make as much money on boats as you can with your business doing well."

"It's not just about money," I replied. "And besides, it isn't intended to replace my business, only to supplement it. I could do boat deliveries and run charters on weekends. That sort of thing. All fun." No matter, though; she was still skeptical.

So I maxed out what was left of a credit card and signed up for a full-time course in the spring at Massachusetts Maritime Academy. I went to class every day for nearly three weeks; studied hard; plotted courses on paper charts; re-learned how to spend hours focused in a classroom, a place I had not known since college; smelled the cool salt air blowing in from Buzzard's Bay in the morning on my way in and saw the cadets marching around the campus. It reminded me of my days as a young man going through basic training at the Coast Guard training base in Cape May. I felt energized, invigorated, and the clean, military feel of the Academy's campus made me feel, sometimes, dizzily caught between my past and the present, eerily intersecting, young again but for some reason trotting around in a pudgy old body.

I watched tugs and barges cruising up and down the Cape Cod Canal, right by the Academy campus, imagining that now I, too, could be a part of that scene, the skipper on the bridge, even though I knew that my license, once I earned it, would only qualify me to operate a vessel a fraction of the size of those craft. Indeed, this realization was driven home to me by my wife, in spades; she, being ever the optimist, suggested that I would ultimately be hired only to captain rickety outboard-motor fishing boats full of obnoxious drunks for a day here or a day there, or to 'deliver' trashy broken-down sailboats from one mooring to another, alone, ingloriously, and for dirt money. She made it sound as attractive to me as cleaning an oily bilge with a toothbrush, or worse, being a glorified drink-server on a yacht full of sleazy chain-smokers. "Don't think you're going to wear a white uniform with gold braid and be Captain of the Love Boat," she advised.

But the process of obtaining a Master's license from the U.S. Coast Guard is a complicated one, requiring letters, affidavits, drug testing, medical examinations, and much more. When I finally had the Master's 100-ton License in my hand, a document that listed me as qualified for 'motor, sail, or steam (imagine – steam! Images of side-wheel steamers of yesteryear churned ahead through the waters of my mind's eye), I was excited and wanted to show the little orange booklet that looked oddly like a passport to everybody. It had mattered a great deal to me to obtain it, because it was a positive accomplishment for me after so many disappointing setbacks in recent times. I wanted to prove to myself that I could study, pass exams, and succeed in an academic endeavor, and when I scored well on my exams, I drove home feeling very emotional and moist-eyed. I had needed a win, and I knew that I had done it all by myself.

But now it was the end of the summer and in Rhode Island, any seasonal boating jobs were closing down for the year. My many inquiries usually ended with "Sounds good, drop me a line in the spring." I wasn't expecting much business over the winter – I would have to head well south for that, to Florida or beyond – but I would have been happy to get something before the New England winter put a stop to all but the big commercial traffic out on the sound.

Unbelievable luck visited me; an old friend and boat-broker, Greg, phoned me one day and asked me if I could handle a boat delivery. It was a short trip; he and a partner had bought, for cheap money, and old Beneteau sailboat, 34 feet long, and planned to 'flip it' fairly quickly, but they needed me to bring it from its slip at a marina in Greenwich Bay, Rhode Island, to their marina in Fall River, Mass., a distance of perhaps twenty miles, a few hours of motoring. They were simply too busy to take the time to do it. The destination marina was also home port to my friend's brokerage. The boat could be serviced, stored, and sold from there. What would I charge, I was asked. "Oh heck," I replied, anxious for a day on the water. "Fifty bucks, OK?" The proposed fee was cheerfully accepted.

Greg's partner, Bill, drove me to the marina in East Greenwich on a warm September Saturday morning, and we boarded the boat and prepared her for sea, so to speak. The day was bright, sunny with puffy little clouds, and calm. Bill was in a hurry to get out of there and get back to work; but we had to get the boat's little Volvo diesel going before he could leave it to me. The sails were not on the spars, and it seemed as though the boat had been there for a rather long time. Wherever one of the dirty, chafed dock lines hung partially in the water, it was covered with a hefty growth of green slime and sea-vegetables.

We cranked the engine until the batteries were almost dead, but the tired little diesel wouldn't start. My heart sank. Oh hell, I thought, this is a bad omen for my first delivery. But at long last, with barely more than a turn left in the batteries, one of the engine's two pistons began firing; at first very slowly, as though it would take forever to build up any RPM, and I thought every moment that it was on the verge of stalling; but at last the other kicked in, and I felt confident to leave the dock. I saw Bill wave back at me as his pickup truck roared away across the marina parking lot. I was on my own; so I cast off the lines, backed out of the slip, and started on my way.

Wisely, so I thought, I had brought a ditty-bag with everything that I figured I might conceivably need that an unknown boat might not have. This included binoculars; a chart of the bay; handheld compass; rain jacket; handheld VHF marine radio; pistol and flares; inflatable life jacket; water bottle and snacks; and my little camera. This habit of thinking ahead served me well, because on that short trip I learned the first big lesson of being a boat delivery skipper; that more often than not, you will not be delivering fully-equipped luxury yachts in Bristol condition, but rather deficient clunkers with engines that don't run right, toilets that don't work, missing electronics, and weird rigs that have been rigged wrong and cause more problems than they provide wind propulsion.

Nevertheless, I brought my charge to the destination dock safely that afternoon after an uneventful few hours, was paid my fee plus a tip, and Bill bought me a few cold beers at the floating Tiki bar at the marina. As I took a few moments to savor the beer and the warm end-of-summer afternoon, I thought, this isn't bad at all, really. What could be better than spending a day on the water in someone else's boat and being paid for it too?

But if I thought that was a lucky break, an even greater opportunity was in store. A lady captain friend, Dana, working long hours on a bay rescue and tow boat patrol, called me a couple of weeks later, really 'out of the blue', saying that she had been asked to skipper a weekend sailing charter on the next Saturday out of Newport, but was simply too busy, and would I be willing to do it? I was excited, and delighted; why of course I would!

"Three businessmen want to go sailing for a 48-hour charter, it begins Friday morning" Captain Dana said. "The boat will be at the dock at Fort Adams, waiting for them and for you. So will the owner of the boat, the charter company that they have contracted with. None of them are sailors, so it's up to you. They want to go overnight to Block Island."

"Block Island?"

"Friday night. They want to go out to dinner, you know, a business meeting sort of thing."

I thanked Dana, but my heart sank. It was now off-season, late in the year and the weather in New England can be quickly changeable offshore, and can make for rough going. Also, the only restaurants that would be open would be those in the village at Old Harbor, on the east side of the island – a good mile or more walk from the New Harbor anchorage on the west side, down dark roads, unless taxis were still in service. Block Island essentially shuts down after Labor Day; launch service stops for the most part, shoreside restaurants in New Harbor are shuttered. We would be fairly alone in a large, cold, dark, windy harbor, at night, a long way from the warmly lighted glow of the National hotel and other hospitality on the Old Harbor waterfront.

"They also want to spent Friday and Saturday night at the island, come back on Sunday. The charter is forty-eight hours; it begins at 10a.m. on Friday and ends at 10 a.m. on Sunday, with the boat back at the Newport dock," Dana said.

"Well then, there is no way that they can spend Saturday night at Block Island" I said, "because it takes four to five hours, depending on the wind, to get back to Newport from the island. We would have to leave on Saturday night or Sunday morning in the wee hours to be back by ten a.m., and I have no idea what conditions will be like."

"Oh, believe, me, I know," she answered, "but that's something that you're going to have to work out with them." It was obvious to me that the fellows who were planning to go sailing didn't really have any idea of the time and distance considerations involved, particularly the vagaries of planning a sailing weekend. With a sailboat, you plan a route, you plan destinations, but you do not plan a rigid schedule, since that is largely unpredictable due to variations in weather, winds, and currents. One may sail downwind from point A to point B with the wind behind, at a steady pace, and arrive at B in X number of hours. But if the wind is from ahead and you must beat to windward in a zig-zag course to reach B, you can almost double your time, X, or worse if the current or tide has turned against you, and winds are light. Then it's time to kick in the motor if you have one. But your schedule will still be different.

Now in simplest terms, people who want to charter a boat for a weekend simply contact a charter company – one that owns a number of boats in a certain area – and leases them out for the weekend. If the people chartering the boat are not good sailors, or familiar with the waters to be sailed, the charter company will put a licensed captain aboard, at extra cost to the charter customers, and also to satisfy the boat's insurance company. So I was soon talking to David, the owner of Sea Adventure Charters, and also the office manager, Doreen, at the company where the three gentlemen worked. I explained to her that in the off season, two nights in Block Island might turn out to be unpleasant, and besides, there was no way that I could have the boat back in Newport on Sunday morning if they spent Saturday night out there. They could pay extra for extra time, but they did not want to do that.

It was soon agreed that instead of such an impossible itinerary, we would spend two days sailing around the bay and in Rhode Island Sound, and that the gentlemen could instead go to dinner in Newport, which abounds in fine restaurants and is easily accessible. I said to Doreen, "The gentlemen will have their cars right on the pier at Fort Adams; we can stay on a mooring nearby that's owned by the charter company. I'll bring them in to the dock in the dinghy after a day of sailing, and they can simply drive into town, not a mile distant, to a leisurely dinner. Then I'll pick them up at the dock when they return and bring them back out to the boat. On top of that, I will take them out for two full, glorious days of sailing in perfect fall weather, as has been predicted." Doreen felt this was a swell idea, and all parties agreed on the more prudent 'float plan' that I had suggested.

Down at the dock, it was a rather windy day, with frequent cool gusts out of the Northwest. The sun was still strong, and the sky as blue and clear and deep as one could possibly wish. It was going to be a beautiful mid-October day. I met David down at the dock; he was a tall, friendly New Zealander with a neat Kiwi accent, which is akin to a British accent though smoother and more mellifluous. I stepped aboard his boat, a 40-foot C&C cruising sloop, which was aptly named Sea Adventure. "What are the names of your other charter boats?" I asked, thinking that there must be some variety in the assignation of names. "This is the only one" he grinned. Oh gosh, I thought, he's a one-boat charter company. Well then I'd best not sink this one.

"Are the clients here yet?" I asked. He looked at me oddly, as if I had used a strange word; I was using my usual marketing business language, and not having been a captain before, I was not sure if it were proper to adopt a gruff tone instead and snarl "Them lubberly polliwoggin' assholes crawl down here yet?" I was thinking that I should opt for the more prudent course and try to make a decent and respectable first impression, especially if I ever wanted this charter boat owner to call me up again when he needed a hired skipper.

"Ah, should be here soon, I guess," he replied, and then began showing me everything there was to know about the boat with dizzying speed - almost as if he expected me to already know most of it – every breaker, switch, cover for this, access to that, thing-to-do-before-doing-something-else, the whole drill. I wondered how I would ever remember everything. I pretended to be soaking every-thing in, as if he were simply giving me a refresher about how to run my own boat. The electrical system was tricky and complex; I despaired of ever memorizing all of it, but instead quietly hoped that his batteries were strong enough that I would not kill them before I could get his boat back to the dock.

Some things, I noticed, were not completely right, or were jury-rigged. A puff of wind nearly took off my cap. I looked at the puzzling array of lines on the end of the boom. "If we have to reef the main, what sort of arrangement do you have for that here?" I asked. He waved dismissively at it, "Oh, ha, well there's some work

I have to do with that, don't worry about it, there's no reefing, not just now." I felt a funny sinking feeling in the pit of my stomach. If you can't 'reef' a sail, or make it smaller in area in strengthening winds, you and your boat can get in serious trouble.

Kiwi Dave and I had barely finished "orientation" when three gentlemen pulled up to the dock in two cars, and began unloading boxes and duffel bags. My goodness, I thought, they look like they've brought a week's worth of food and clothing at the very least. Boxes came aboard, an entire box of bottles of wine, a box of nothing but various types of fruit, presumably to ward off scurvy; a box of bread, salad dressing and fixings, a case of beer, a case of water bottles, in short, enough supplies for an extended cruise. I made no comment in that regard, but cheerfully helped bring the luggage and supplies below.

Friendly introductions were soon made. The leader of the group, George, was a short, heavyset man in his late fifties, the owner of the manufacturing company to which they all belonged, and a man who had the odor of money about him, his clothes of only the best make and quality from his windbreaker down to his boat shoes; everything he wore also seemed new. He had, as he later explained, grown up poor in Greece, immigrated to the United States as a young man and through hard work, self-improvement, and dogged industriousness, he had become a businessman of considerable success and property, and he had also acquired a good education. He was an earnest, warm, and very smart self-made man, passionately spoken in any matter he chose to discuss.

Second in command was Dick, the eldest of the group, in his early sixties, a true Massachusetts Yankee, old-school manufacturing sort, machinist by trade, thin, wiry and weathered, pleasant and practical, not especially talkative but friendly enough.

The junior member of the group was Tony, a sharp, serious, dark-haired and clean-cut young man with black square framed glasses. Tony was in his mid-twenties, a talented lad of third-generation immigrant Italian stock, who was learning to be a plant manager under George's tutelage. Tony was an able cook (he did the cooking and meal-planning for the trip) and also made his own wine – which he brought along – and it was excellent wine, at that. Tony seemed always eager to please, nervous about his status, and anxious to fit into his place and do everything correctly. He was meticulous and prompt in his preparation of fresh food and sandwiches, which he seemed to have a talent for, and particularly good taste in his selection of ingredients. But he was also, it seemed to me, very 'uptight', and so I was very careful, throughout the trip, not to inadvertently give offense, or to be overly critical, as I suspected that he would exact revenge for any slight, real or imagined, sealing me up in the bilge perhaps with a cask of his own Amontillado.

George, by his own admission, had owned some large yachts in his time – but they were power yachts, and he had not done a great deal more than steer them briefly, at any one time, under the watchful eye of the hired Captain. Dick had sailed, all right, and had sailed New England waters too, but the largest boat he had sailed had been a 'Laser', which is a very small, albeit fast, one-person racing eggshell with a single triangle of a sail not terribly larger than a bed-sheet. Tony told us quite matter-of-factly that he had never sailed at all, and he demonstrated the truth of his statement later in the trip when he was given a 'trick at the wheel' for a spell.

We prepared to leave the dock; just before we shoved off, David took me aside; "Good show, talking them out of the Block Island thing. Have a safe time and really wear them out." I was not especially clear about what he meant by this, but there was no time to ask for clarification.

The wind had piped up smartly now out of the Northwest. When we left Newport harbor, there were whitecaps on the bay and the wind was blowing around twenty to twenty-five knots. The men were seated in the ample cockpit, grinning, excited, anxious for a good time, and jaunty. George shouted something to the other two about some prior adventure down in the Caribbean where it had been blowing and the skipper "had laid her right over." At that moment a dark cloud blew over and obscured the sun; the waters turned steel-gray. "Hey Mike, let's take this thing out and lay her right over, ha, ha" George said. "Put up all the sails!" He was making me nervous. I was steering. There were a number of large sailing vessels, including two day-charter schooners, tacking back and forth through the choppy waters of this congested passage between Newport and Jamestown; it was a moving obstacle course. A powerful gust slewed the bow of Sea Adventure off course even though we were motoring.

The boat had two sails – the main, which could not be reefed, and a roller-furling Genoa, a big foresail like an oversized jib. It would provide plenty of thrust in this wind, and be easy to control and reduce in size, on my own if I had to. "We're just going to fly the genny for now," I told George. "Tony, want to help? Those lines over there."

Tony looked perplexed; Dick, seeing this, went over to the winch, grabbed the handle out of pocket; he knew what to do. I directed George to the furling halyard; "Release that slowly and in a controlled manner when I tell you," I said. George looked a little disappointed. "If it's not enough, George, we can hoist the main as well, but let's run with just the jenny first and see how she does," I said, sensing his disappointment. As he stood up, George whacked his head on the outer support brace of the cockpit's dodger. It was too low. He glared at it. "Why is that so low, like that?" he complained, rubbing his head.

The big 140 Genoa rolled out, filled with wind, and *Sea Adventure* sprang to life, leaned into it, accelerated, and took off like a shot across the water, gradually hardening up to beat to windward up Narragansett Bay. "Where are we going?" George asked. "I thought we were going to Block Island for the day."

"With these winds there will be six-foot seas out there, it's all the way downwind, and then we will have to beat against them for more than twenty miles just to get back here" I replied. "You won't get back here until very late, well past dinner time, if you even want to eat by then. Today we stay in the bay; I will give you the Grand Tour. Tomorrow, with the winds predicted to back around to the southwest, I will take you out there, and we will sail home with the wind behind us, a comfortable run home." George had a skeptical look on his face. At that moment there was a big gust of wind and I deliberately bore away to leeward so that the puff caught the jenny full and laid the boat right over so that the rail was awash. The men quickly grabbed onto anything fixed so that they would not end up in a pile on the lee lifelines, but then roared with delight; they loved it, and George, momentarily startled, nodded his head in agreement, since he had been on the windward side of the cockpit and had to grab hold of a winch very quickly. "Stay in the bay, then, this is good," he acknowledged. I knew then that I had what I wanted, but had it good and hard.

The sun came out again, and we enjoyed a great sail up the bay toward Providence. I played the role of tour guide, pointing out the many geographical sites and sights, Warwick Light, the Aldrich Mansion, islands and the like, until early afternoon, when we rounded the north end of Prudence Island, Providence Point, and turned south to return to Newport. Even though it was later in the afternoon, they wanted to stop for lunch, so we went into the now-empty Potter's Cove on the east side of Prudence Island, picked up a mooring, and lighted the gas grill that was mounted on the stern rail.

It was a beautiful afternoon. The clarity of the air was remarkable; dry and cool, and, as my pilot friend Joe says, "clear in a million." The tall grasses along the shore of the cove were yellowing from summer's green, a sure sign of fall. The wind only darkened the surface of the cove as williwaws, coming over the island from the west, descended and made cat's paws on its sheltered surface. Dick grilled steaks, Tony made a great salad, and George opened a bottle of Tony's red wine. We raised the cockpit table and ate, for George had graciously invited me to sit with them. We toasted the week-end, and then as the sundry table items were cleared to the galley below, we cast off and sailed for Newport, with the now-westerly wind abeam or on a close reach. Clearing the southern tip of Prudence Island, we now felt the wind strongly anew; spray from the choppy waters danced aboard and shamelessly splashed the dodger. Near sunset we were at the entrance to the harbor; we furled up the Genoa, started the engine, and with the light that was left, I took them for a slow circumnavigation of crowded, colorful Newport harbor before going to the mooring that Kiwi Dave had told me was available.

In a little while, just around dark, the men emerged from the cabin down below, now dressed in their business suits, ready to go ashore for dinner. I thought the change of clothes odd; they were, after all, staying on a boat for the weekend, and in Newport, during the yachting season, one need not wear a suit to dine in most places because, after all, one has been yachting. In fact, if you're dressed in a suit, it's a sure sign that you haven't been out boating at all, unless it has been on one of those mega-yachts where the closest one gets to salt water is a distant view through tinted mega-windows, where one is so far removed from the weather and the sea that there is no need for boating attire at all. You're not really boating, after all if instead of wiggling your toes in the chilly water of a drenched cockpit, you're wiggling them in a plush deep-pile dry carpet.

I helped them board the inflatable runabout, started up the engine, and dutifully motored them in to the dock, near their cars.

"Call my cell phone when you get back" I said, "And I'll be here to pick you up. Do you know, ballpark, when you might be back here?"

"Oh, we won't be late," George said.

"That's good," I said, "because the weather radio says that a front is going to come through tonight with a lot of wind, later. I wouldn't want to be trying to run a dinghy around in the dark once that pipes up."

"Oh, but we are very sheltered in here, yes?"

"I hope so."

I had seen a dark band of clouds, very high up in the atmosphere, to the northwest, stretching from horizon to horizon, just as the sun was setting. A powerful cold front was forecast to roll through late that evening, bringing with it high winds. From the look of the sky, some weather was definitely on the way. I just hoped that my intrepid jaunty yachtsmen would be back before the fun started. Then I thought how fortunate we were to be on a mooring that night rather than riding on an anchor in Block Island's lonely exposed harbor.

But now there was nothing to do. Properly, I should remain with the boat. But after all, it was on its owner's mooring. There was no dinner, and I dare not rifle through my guests' goods to furnish myself; I had no idea what meal-planning Tony had done, and I did not want to arouse his wrath by eating something that he might have plans for, a choice morsel intended for someone's gullet other than mine. Yet, I was hungry; and my pickup truck was sitting patiently parked on the pier. So I motored over to the dock, secured the dinghy, and drove into Newport to my favorite Irish pub in the town for a generous portion of fish and chips, a pint of Guinness, and an hour of football on the big TV above the bar.

I had been back to the boat nearly an hour when my phone jingled. Somehow I knew that they were coming, and had already begun motoring toward the dock when I saw the bluish headlights of George's BMW winding down the long dark road to the pier. I was waiting for them, and helped them aboard, all three of them happy, laughing, and reeking of Martinis and red wine. Luckily, I got them aboard without anyone falling into the water. My long association with boats, bars, booze, and benumbed sailing buddies had prepared me well for this job, I thought. Dick and Tony stumbled below after jolly good-nights, but George wanted to sit up in the cockpit for awhile to talk. He was pleasantly, happily mellowed by the drink, and talkative; he looked up at the clear, star-studded sky and spoke about his boyhood in Greece, growing up in a village right on the shores of the Aegean, a village so poor that there was no electricity, so there were no streetlights at night and the stars were bright and beautiful. I began to truly appreciate this man of poetic instinct, and was sorry when he finally went below to turn in. I stayed up for awhile and then retired below.

Sea Adventure had a large 'owner's cabin' aft under the cockpit, the most luxurious in the craft, essentially a queen-size bed, and this was George's private cabin. Dick, the eldest, got the Vee-berth up forward, also private, usually referred to as the guest cabin. That left two curved settees on either side of the main cabin's folding dinette table. Tony of course took the larger one, intended to serve as a single berth in a pinch; I got the settee that was designed to be a settee and not a bed and was not very large nor wide nor really intended to be slept on, but I made the best of it, after all they were paying me, but I felt, as I threw a blanket over myself, like a servant rather than a Captain, but there was no other option, really. It was not my ship; it was theirs. But at least they had Tony to clean up the dishes, make the sandwiches, and fetch the liquor. I suppressed evil thoughts of resentment, and soon fell asleep.

It seemed as though I had been asleep for only an instant, when all Hell broke loose. I awoke to the sound of terrible wind – blowing a full gale – that had apparently descended upon the harbor like a thunderbolt. It came right out of the North – dead North – the only point of the compass from which Brenton Cove, the place where we were moored, was not superbly protected. Now, winds of forty knots or more were funneling down the bay right into the cove. The boat was actually swinging on her mooring, and at times heeling, first to port, then starboard; seas kicked up in the cove – real seas – and she began plunging and pitching on her mooring. Loose halyards rang and clanged angrily against the aluminum mast. They were high up on the mast and there was little that could be done in the darkness and madly rocking and gyrating boat. I was used to the sound, in some ways, even though I hated it, because at the time I owned a fiberglass loop with an aluminum mast. And while an aluminum mast is an excellent support for modern rigging, it is also a wonderfully efficient transmitter of sound, and the standing part of the mast that bisected the cabin, from the overhead to the cabin sole, was a perfect loudspeaker, bringing the horrendous cacophony of all that was amiss in the 40-odd feet of vertical darkness above into the main cabin in high-fidelity.

The three men were worried; I went topside, held on, and inspected the boat in the darkness as truly cold wind buffeted me. All was in order, despite the awful conditions; the mooring painter was well secured and wrapped in chafing gear. There was nothing to do but ride it out. I went below. The wind blew stronger. I lay back down. The guys could not sleep, though. Tony was worried that we might sink. At one point, even George went up into the cockpit. He thought we had broken loose from the mooring. The clanging of halyards whipping about against the mast – and the humming of the wind in the standing rigging, the stays – was loud and constant. But I drifted back off to sleep. At one point, after a particularly jolting lurch, I awakened somewhat, though not completely, and realized that if the boat should break free, she would be ashore, on the sandy beach to leeward, in moments; there was nothing to be done, the shore was too close, the harbor too crowded in the dark to try to maneuver, and the storm too furious. No one would die. The boat, on top of that, was insured. She would probably only sustain cosmetic damage from the beach if she did not swipe anyone else on her way to the steep shoreline. I went back to sleep, because I had ridden out an even worse blow once on an anchor in my old wooden yawl in Vineyard Haven. We were on a secure mooring and were going nowhere. But that did not help these three fellows get back to sleep; they were certain that we were doomed.

In the morning, the wind was still blowing briskly, but it had moderated greatly. I was a bit groggy for not having slept a solid night, but I had slept nonetheless, and I yearned for a hot cup of strong black coffee to awaken body and mind. I emerged into the cockpit to greet a cool, breezy day, much cooler than the day before, but bright, clear, and blue with a solid North wind. It would be a good autumn sailing day, I thought. The front blew through during the night and would blow out by late afternoon, possibly becoming calm and even perhaps shifting around to the Southwest, as the forecaster was predicting. My three jolly tars were slow to get going, though; Tony took awhile to get the coffee on, and then only I really wanted any. I realized that, quite possibly, none of them had slept a wink.

But today was a different day, especially for me. The trepidation of the day before was gone; I had sailed this boat for a full day, knew how she behaved in blustery airs, and felt a new confidence in myself and my ability to handle her. The three guys sat in the cockpit, leaning forward toward the center, hangdog, groggy, quiet. "Well gentlemen," I piped brightly, feeling a bit jaunty, "What adventures are in store for today? Where can I take you?"

George looked up at me, wincing at the brightness of the sun reflecting off the water, and asked, "Can we just stay right here?"

I was quietly aghast; oh my, oh no, this wouldn't do, I reflected. They had paid a price for this charter, I had seen the articles when I signed my page of the contract before we left, and there were still more than 24 hours on the clock. They had to get their money's worth, I thought. Good and hard.

"Oh goodness, you certainly don't want to stay here all day. After all, I did promise to take you offshore today. Upper bay yesterday, out Block Island way today! Now we had best get under way." I turned the key and the diesel engine rumbled to life, puffing white smoke out astern.

There wasn't much breakfast – Tony sent up some fruit (again) and bread. Half my kingdom for just one little egg, or a rasher, or a bit of corned beef hash, I yearned, wistfully. All this fruit and I'll be standing watch in the potty the balance of the afternoon.

We rounded Fort Adams and began our trip out into the sound, past Castle Hill on our port, past distant Beavertail Light on our starboard. It was a truly sparkly day with a good breeze, and once again I rolled out the big Genoa, but there was no talk this time about raising the mainsail, or trying to lay her over to get the lee rail awash. In fact, later, as the wind moderated to a gentle breeze, I offered to raise the main, but George said, "No, I think we are just fine, no need to do that, really."

As I put Point Judith abaft the starboard beam late morning, and all the open Sound lay before us with Block Island clearly visible in the distance, George turned to me and, seeing the bulk of the mainland recede into the distance astern, said, "Hey Mike, there is nothing to see out here. Shouldn't we go someplace where we can see things?" I understood his meaning immediately. So I played along to save face for him.

"Well, you're right, George, and we're still a long way from Block Island. But back there, you can see all the great mansions lining the Newport coastline – is that more what you had in mind? Do you want me to take us back to the coast for a water view of the mansions?"

"Yes, yes!" He replied, "That's a great idea, let's do that!" So I brought the boat about and headed back toward the mainland, where George would be happy and feel, perhaps, a little more secure. When we were only a couple of miles off the land, the wind moderated even more. The airs were light, now, and the seas relatively calm. I invited Tony to take the wheel.

The previous day, George had steered for awhile, and he was a fair helmsman, but did not want to do his 'trick' at the wheel for very long. Dick could also steer, not terribly well (as he was used to a little tiller), but he caught on fast. Tony, though, was another matter. It wasn't as though he were unfamiliar with sailing, no; it was as if he were blind, blind as a clam. At times we would be going 90 degrees off course, and he seemed not to know the difference, even though the land was plainly in sight for a reference. The rest of the time, our wake looked like a meandering river, reminding me of the old Coast Guard Chief who, on my first time at the helm of our ship, had drawled, "Son, there's a (unprintable) snake following this ship." But he did not want to relinquish the helm, and Dick and George were quite happy to let him do his worst as they looked on in pokerfaced amusement. The meanest thing I would allow myself to say, after correcting his awful steering multiple times, was to cheerfully observe that "It's a good thing that we're out here in open water; it's good place to learn to steer because there's nothing to hit."

Finally it was time for Tony to go below and make sandwiches; it was early afternoon, and George said, "Mike, let's head back in now." So I started the motor again, furled the genoa, and we began heading back toward Newport Harbor.

Now, the gentlemen seemed to wake up; they became chatty, happy, animated. They were going home to their hot showers, beds, families, and familiar comforts. They had an hour and a half drive to their homes north of Boston; they would survive that. As soon as we tied up to the dock to unload, they had already packed up all their gear and goods; they paid me, tipped me, and complimented me so kindly and generously that I was, for a few moments, quite sorry to see them go. But I have never seen folks get off a boat so quickly. You'd think that it had been on fire, or that they were rats deserting a sinking ship, although we were hardly sinking by any stretch. Even George was a chubby bundle of perspiring energy, trundling his own overstuffed Pullman bag up the noisy aluminum ramp in double-time, wheels grumbling across the uneven planks of the dock; and then they were gone, a miniature motorcade in a hurry, like JFK headed for Parkland Hospital. I phoned Kiwi Dave; he was across the harbor at the Newport Boat Show, which just happened to be going on that weekend; he would be over in a little while to check the boat over and release me.

For the first time that weekend, the boat was quiet and, oddly, empty. I felt alone. Tony had left me an entire box of nice multi-grain breads, an assortment of premium quality fresh fruit, and a few other items; but of course they had taken all of the wine and beer that was left over. But I was happy with the fruit and bread, it was a bonus. Finally Kiwi Dave showed up, and took a few minutes to make sure that all was in order aboard Sea Adventure.

"Well," he said, "You're released, no need to keep you around now that they have gone home."

"That's swell," I said. "My wife and I were invited to a dinner party this evening at the home of some friends of ours. I was disappointed that I would not be able to go, that she would have to go without me, but now I can. I even have some nice bread and fruit to bring. I guess they didn't want to bother hauling it back."

"They took all their booze, eh?" He laughed.

"Sure, but they tipped me nicely, no issue there."

"Good enough. Any idea why they ended the charter early?"

"Well, I don't think they got much sleep last night with the wind storm. I don't think any of them are used to sleeping in a rocking bed with a horrendous lot of noise going on."

He started to grin, and let out a low, evil, knowing laugh. "But I did take them for two good days of sailing" I offered.

"Did you leave them good and tired, worn out?"

"Oh absolutely" I said. "Although if they had slept last night, we might still be out there right now."

He was laughing. "That's the whole point, you know. Get them good and tired, any way you can, bushed, worn out. That way they feel they've gotten their money's worth."

◆◆◆◆◆◆

Autumn River Cruise on Spray

Captain Slocum came to mind again this past fall, probably because I had been given a rather unique boat delivery job by a yacht broker friend. I was to bring a Bruce Roberts "Spray" up the Taunton River in Massachusetts from a marina in Mount Hope Bay to a boatyard in Dighton, where she would be hauled out for the season. She had just been sold. It would be the second time in the season that I had delivered this same boat from one place to another for this particular friend and customer.

Bruce Roberts-Goodson is a well-known Australian yacht designer who has designed and built many yachts inspired by Captain Joshua Slocum's original Spray, a derelict oyster dredge very similar to the few remaining antique wooden skipjacks on Chesapeake Bay today. Slocum rebuilt Spray and sailed her around the world in 1895, becoming the first person to ever circumnavigate the globe single-handedly. His subsequent account, *Sailing Alone Around the World* became a heart-warming classic.

But Slocum's *Spray* was really a workboat for oyster fishing, sloop-rigged, shoal draft, impossibly beamy. The design is not particularly fast, in my opinion, but the boats are roomy below and good for living aboard or extended cruising. The shallow draft is great for going into bays and rivers, but for blue water sailing, experts disagree. Roberts referred to *Spray* as 'the ultimate cruising boat', which is extremely helpful if you are selling *Spray*-inspired designs; but famed (and controversial) naval historian and architect Howard Chappelle pronounced *Spray* a horrible boat for going off-shore and went so far as to say that the only reason that Slocum and *Spray* stayed 'on top' for so long was because Slocum was an extraordinary mariner.

Some years ago, when I was younger, more idealistic, purist, and clueless, I had the shameless audacity to tell Mr. Roberts-Goodson at a Slocum Society meeting that his 'Sprays' were hardly *Sprays* at all, being designed, some of them, with two masts, hulls made of fiberglass, much longer hulls than Slocum's 38-foot LOA Spray and with different cabin layouts, etc., which reddened his face considerably and made his facial hairs twitch. It was wrong of me to be so impertinent, of course. Indeed, the 33-foot *Spray* that I was now taking upriver – motoring, by the way, into the teeth of a cold northwesterly Autumn blow – had little in common, it seemed at first, with Joshua Slocum's famous vessel. But then, as I once again felt the sluggish mass of her barn-heavy hull beneath my feet, as Denise and I chugged along, I entertained the possibility that perhaps it had more in common with Slocum's dredge than I had initially thought.

Two months earlier, my broker friend had first hired me to bring this boat around to the marina when he had purchased it outright from its previous owner. That delivery began on a mooring in the Warren River, a distance of about twelve nautical miles from where she was now tied to the dock, awaiting the next leg of her journey. My son Tom and I brought her around from Warren that first time, and slow going it was. The bottom was foul, and the three-blade bronze propeller was little more than a barnacle-muffin, essentially; when it spun on its shaft, it generated about as much thrust as a candied apple spinning on its stick.

We motored, we sailed; the day grew hot. We ran out of our shared bottle of water, and grew hungry. Then the wind piped up, and with the big genoa out full, we managed about four knots, going with the help of a 1-knot current. It became an interminable voyage, taking all day, akin to trying to sail a cement barge across a sea of molasses with a handkerchief.

Now, the situation was different. She had been hauled and cleaned and returned to the water. It was late October, with a blustery northwest wind piping up to twenty-five knots and more. There were whitecaps on Mount Hope Bay. It was bright, sunny, and almost cold, and the leaves in the trees along the shore, past foliage peak, were brilliant yellows, reds, and brown, mostly golden.

The boat had been built in the 1970's or 80's in England. Heavy and strong, stable and beamy, she also therefore possessed a great deal of inertia. i.e., once she got some way on her, she was going to keep going. I had no trouble getting off the dock and out of the shelter of the breakwater and into the blustery bay, but unlike the original *Spray* of Captain Slocum, this boat was afflicted with a large tiller. I hate tillers on all but small sailboats, where their advantages of precision and quick control are matched by a small boat's speed and responsiveness. In a large boat they obstruct the cockpit and are tiring for any passage lasting more than an hour or two. No boat greater in length than twenty-five feet ought to be steered with a tiller, and certainly never for offshore passage-making. That is my truly opinionated opinion.

In any event, now under way, we were about to encounter our first and only real obstacle, the Brightman Street Bridge across the Taunton River. This iron drawbridge was built in 1908, the same year that Joshua Slocum disappeared at sea. I do not know whether or not Slocum ever sailed the original *Spray* up the Taunton River. He might have, although there would have been nothing up there for him to see or do. The bridge is low, and I had known in advance that it would have to open for us. I did my homework beforehand and learned that the bridge keeper monitors VHF Channels 16 and 13. I tried him on both, on my hand-held, as we approached the bridge. No answer. Again. No answer. The tidal current was with us, surging us toward the bridge. Fortunately I had obtained the telephone number for the keeper's station on the bridge. I gave Denise the number and she called on her cell phone (I was busy managing the stubborn tiller), and he answered the phone. He apologized; he'd had the VHF radio volume turned way down. I silently wondered why. Perhaps so that the occasional crackle would not interrupt the mid-day soap opera on his portable TV, I imagined, or maybe a game show.

He asked Denise, who was still on the phone with him, what the name of our boat was. Denise looked up, squinting. "What's our boat's name?" She asked. I thought for a moment. I had not looked at the transom before leaving the dock. "*Spray*," I replied, which she relayed.

"OK, *Spray*," he responded, and the bridge began to open.

Later at the dock in Dighton, she looked at the transom as we disembarked, and saw that the name of the boat was the 'Cyndi Jo' or something like that. She was aghast; she had believed that the boat's name was actually *Spray*, and couldn't believe that she had given a fake name to the bridge operator.

"We had to tell him something," I said, "He only wanted a name so that he could put it into his log. I'm sure that every time he opens that bridge he has to log it."

She thought it was funny that I had made up the name on the spot, but what else was I to do? "It was all I could think of at the moment," I told her, "And it wasn't completely a lie anyway."

Our little trip, with the incoming tide, took us much less time than expected. We sailed past lovely, quaint little Somerset Village, a well-kept secret, and narrowing riverbanks lined with tall, yellowing eelgrass and colorful trees shedding their leaves under a deep sapphire sky.

We had left a car at the destination boatyard in Dighton; so once we had the boat secured to the floating dock, with ample fenders and spring lines set, we reluctantly said good-bye to her. That's one of the greatest perks of the delivery Captain business; you get a few hours to cruise on someone else's boat, perhaps on a lovely day, up a river, call it even a 'fall foliage cruise', and at the end of it all you not only just walk away, but you get paid for it, too.

Denise had packed a little picnic lunch; a couple of sandwiches, chips and cookies, and a thermos of tea. Two little personal-sized bottles of wine and cups were included for when we finally reached the dock and tied up; we could each have a glass of wine and toast the day, the trip, the Autumn, the bittersweet end of the boating season in New England.

Before we left the yard, I took a few moments to check things out down below, to make sure that the breakers were off, that there was no water in the bilge, nothing unusual going on, while Denise went to the car to wait. It was quiet down below, late afternoon golden sun slanting in through the cabin portlights, ripples lapping dully against the hull, slap-slap of a loose halyard somewhere above. I peered into the darkness at the starboard quarter-berth, and chuckled as I remembered going to a party a week earlier where an old friend of mine, John from Edinburgh, reminded me of my little prank some years earlier when there was a major Joshua Slocum exhibit at the Whaling Museum in New Bedford. There had been a half-cabin life-size mock-up of Slocum's aft cabin on the original *Spray*, complete with a bookshelf, his Martini-Henry rifle mounted on the bulkhead, and a bunk with a straw-filled mattress, thin, covered with white and blue-striped old-fashioned mattress ticking, in full view. It had been re-created from Slocum's own drawings and the illustrations in Sailing Alone.

Somehow, I could not help myself; no others besides me and my friends were there, so I ducked under the ropes, ignored the signs, and climbed into the berth, spending a few moments in Joshua Slocum's bunk, much to their astonishment and amusement. For a moment or two, anyway, that was as close to being Captain Slocum as I would ever get.

Now, as I looked around at this unkempt cabin in need of real sprucing-up, I wished the old girl good fortune, new life, and many safe sea-miles in her future, and luck and perseverance to her new owner, whoever he or she might be. Then it was time, reluctantly, to go.

◆◆◆◆◆◆◆

Hunting Pirate Treasure

The wind has suddenly piped up, freshening quickly out of the south. Captain Barry Clifford, scowling behind his sunglasses, shakes his head, and signals to the crew, with some obvious disappointment, that it's time to head for home. Adding to the anxiety is the knowledge that a hurricane named IRENE is churning around in the ocean somewhere to the south, heading this way. There are preparations to be made.

A swell has begun to pick up, and the research vessel Vast Explorer strains at her spider-web of six anchors holding her off the beach on the exposed ocean side of Cape Cod. It's too bad; in the past few hours, divers have brought up stacked silver Spanish coins – a sign that they were in cloth bags, according to Barry; a couple of concretions that may be cannon balls encased in cemented sand and pebbles; tiny gleaming nodules of African gold dust; and intriguing solid silver knobs that once capped the scroll-ends of rolled charts in the Captain's cabin, the first such artifacts that Barry's expedition has ever found. All of the silver is the color of barbecue charcoal – not quite black, not quite gray, but – charcoal.

It's getting late in the afternoon on this warm August day. One of the divers, Jeff, a tall man, braces against the wind and the motion of the ship and grins. He's been diving with Barry for years. "Yup, whenever we start finding stuff – every time – old Bellamy starts blowin' his horn!"

He's referring to Captain Samuel Bellamy – known as 'Black Sam Bellamy' – the notorious English pirate who ran his treasure-laden ship Whydah ashore in a howling April nor-easter in 1717 right beneath us. Only a few survived – not including the colorful, charismatic Bellamy – only to be hanged as pirates not long after. The crew of the *Vast Explorer* is matter-of-factly convinced that Bellamy haunts the site, and that his bones lie below. Indeed, bones – human remains – have been found by Barry's Expedition *Whydah* divers and crew over the years.

Bellamy had plundered more than 50 ships before heading north, quite probably with the intention of meeting up with his lover, Maria Hallett, and sailing on together to Maine.

The *Whydah* – formerly a slave ship, and named for an African bird - was Bellamy's biggest prize. It was a 300-ton English slave ship that had just finished the second leg of the Atlantic slave trade on its second voyage and was loaded with a fortune in gold, silver, and precious trade goods. Bellamy converted the captured *Whydah*, outfitting his new flagship as a 28-gun raiding vessel (upgraded from its original 18 guns), set sail northwards along the eastern coast of North America.

But *Whydah* was swept up in a hurricane-force storm at midnight on April 26, sailing too close in the darkness to the outer arm of Cape Cod, and was driven onto sand bar shoals in 16 feet of water some 500 feet from the coast of what is now Wellfleet, Mass. Shortly before midnight, the masts snapped and drew the heavily loaded ship into 30 feet of water where she capsized and quickly sank, taking Bellamy and all but two of the *Whydah's* 149-man crew with her. One hundred and two bodies were known to have washed ashore and were buried by the town coroner, leaving the others unaccounted for. The castaways were captured and prosecuted for piracy in Boston, and six were hanged in October. Two were set free, the court believing their testimony that they had been forced into piracy.

In 1984, Bellamy became famous again when the wreckage of the *Whydah* was finally discovered, the first confirmed pirate ship recovered in U.S. waters in modern times. At the time of its sinking, the *Whydah* was the largest pirate prize captured in the West Indies in the 18th century, and the treasure in its hold included huge quantities of indigo, ivory, gold, and over 30,000 pounds sterling (approximately 4.5 to 5 tons).

The discovery of the wreck was made in July 1984 by a diving crew led by underwater explorer Barry Clifford. In 1985, Clifford recovered the ship's bell upon which were the words "THE WHY-DAH GALLY 1716," and subsequently founded The *Whydah* Pirate Museum on MacMillan Wharf in Provincetown, Mass., dedicated to Samuel Bellamy and the *Whydah*. It houses many artifacts which were recovered from the actual wreck, including a sealed cannon whose contents, as revealed by fiber-optic examination, appeared to include coins, gold and jewelry. A portion of the roughly 200,000 artifacts so far recovered are currently on a six-year tour around the United States under the sponsorship of The National Geographic Society. The tour is titled "Real Pirates" and more can be learned at www.whydah.com. The tour, according to Chris Macort, director of operations for Expedition Whydah, is well worth seeing: "All the best of the treasures that we have found – including the ship's bell – is on that tour. It's really not something to miss."

I signed on with Barry, his crew, and the 105-ton research vessel *Vast Explorer* on the advice of a friend who introduced me to the legendary Barry Clifford. It was an unusual part-time summer job, to be sure. Hard work, and long hours serving as deckhand, engineer, even cook, once; but it was one of the most exciting jobs I've ever had, working with the divers and marine archaeologists and being one of the first to see the treasure and artifacts brought up.

On expedition, the *Vast* goes out to the wreck site where a strategically-positioned network of anchors have been positioned, and ties up to them like a spider in the center of a web. Winches are used to jog the vessel around a few feet at a time to precisely locate the stern of the ship over a specific area. The *Vast* has been equipped with a custom-designed prop wash deflector that, when lowered into position, directs the stream of thrust from her twin screws directly downward where literally tons of sand are removed in a matter of only a few hours. The *Vast's* engines are so powerful that when engaged in gear, the stern of the vessel actually lifts up a couple of feet from the force of the downward thrust. The entire vessel vibrates, and plumes of dense sandy water can be seen welling to the surface yards away.

This is necessary because the *Whydah's* treasure isn't on the surface of the bottom. It's buried many feet down – from 20 to 40 feet - under three centuries of sand deposited from the eroding cliffs of Cape Cod. When the *Whydah* wrecked, she was very close to the actual shoreline at the time. So Barry and the VAST have to blast away many feet of sand to get down to the cobbles of the original beach before they can start finding the treasure that has percolated downward. Barry has studied the Ice Age geology of the Cape – his well-thumbed books on the subject are in a rack in the main saloon belowdecks – so each day is a sequence of "blowing," then diving – divers are equipped with custom-designed metal detectors and magnetometers – and jogging the *Vast* around a few feet at a time to follow leads and signals detected by the divers. Barry knows what he is doing – his carefully annotated charts of the wreck site are no less than an archaeologist's drawing of a wreck site grid, showing where cannons and artifacts have been found, drawn in, drawn to scale, against the outline of the overturned hull of the wreck. Much of the documentation is photographic, with still photos and underwater video taken by Barry's son Brandon Clifford, who is also a professional for Olympus as an underwater cameraman. Brandon has been diving around the world with Barry since he was a kid, and Barry never leaves a location (or 'pit') until Brandon has thoroughly inspected it with detector or hand held magnetometer and gives the thumbs up that the pit is "clean."

On one such occasion in 2007, hearing something deeply buried beneath a location that was supposed to have been completely excavated 1985, Brandon discovered the cannon pile, which was 10 feet deeper than the same site where cannons were excavated in 1985. The question remains: what's buried deeper? This is why the *Vast* and Expedition *Whydah* have returned to this location, Barry emphasizes.

A system of precise DGPS receivers mounted directly over the deflector – dead nuts over the hole being dug – help Barry position the VAST precisely. But before anyone dives, the engines are shut down completely for safety. Then the divers get to work. The principal diver wears a suit equipped with pumped hot water and air supplied from the deck. It's not deep water, but it is cold, not much above freezing. Without the hot-water suit, a diver gets chilled in less than half an hour. With the hot water suit, a diver can work for two hours or more on the wreck site.

The *Vast Explorer* remains anchored on site, in view of the beaches of the Cape Cod National Seashore, for several days at a time. We work from first light – grab your coffee and drink it fast – until dusk. Then the crew is treated to a meal often cooked by Capt. Barry himself, who clearly enjoys cooking, and is a very able fellow in the galley. We crewmembers clean up afterwards, always cautioned in the art of cleaning the captain's treasured black cast iron pans – the secret to a good meal – and especially how NOT to clean them!

We take turns on different days whipping up lunch for the crew. The deck is a busy place midday, and the divers and crewmen barely have time to eat, but it's hard work in cold water, and they need to eat. The divers, who include Barry's son Brandon Clifford, not only search for the treasure but document it carefully as well, using underwater cameras and cameras on deck and in the conservation lab area. Barry doesn't like the term "treasure hunter." He insists that his work is more marine archaeology, but won't deny that finding pirate treasure brings a twinkle to his eye after all. But there is no pirate treasure gift shop; the *Whydah* treasure is on tour, and in the museum, which seems to me a living classroom, teaching thousands of people around the world every year what 'real' pirates from the Golden Age of Piracy were actually like. This is part of Barry's mission. And the mission continues, since quite nearly four tons of silver remain buried somewhere in the wreck site.

Perhaps the most intriguing thing, to me, is the image of Bellamy with a pistol in his belt, wrapped in red silk. This is part of the Bellamy legend, surviving from eyewitness accounts of him. The preservative effects of sand and silt have allowed *Expedition Whydah* to find and conserve actual pieces of fabric from the wreck. Some years ago, they also brought up the remains of a pistol – partially wrapped in a few remnants of red silk. At night, on the ship, I lie in my bunk thinking, in the darkness, of how I am sleeping anchored over the graves of Captain Bellamy and some of his crew, entombed beneath yards of sand and many feet of cold seawater. Indeed, the Expedition has brought up wood from the ship, carefully preserved by the smothering blanket of sand and silt.

Many of the cannon brought to the surface were fully loaded – powder and ball – with the wooden tompions, or plugs, still in the muzzle. There were many cannon aboard – more than the *Whydah* could use, and probably plundered from other vessels, since they were valuable, but why fully loaded? Intriguingly, Chris Macort says that powder retrieved from these cannons, when fully dried out, will still flash when touched with an open flame, even after nearly three centuries underwater.

During the night, while we sleep, the VAST rolls a little, and it's like being at sea in many ways, perhaps because we are. We are not sheltered at all from the ocean, which means that Barry needs to remain vigilant for weather changes since we are so close to shore. When it's time to leave, the anchor lines are buoyed and dropped, with the exception of the bow anchor, which is raised. Then we head home, two and a half hours away around the curled upper arm of the Cape.

So now we're heading into port for the last time this season. Captain Barry hands out responsibilities and privileges carefully and slowly. You don't get a new increment of responsibility until he is sure that you have earned it. On this last trip of the season, Barry gives me the privilege of nearly two hours of wheel time – I think

I had 15 minutes at the helm the first trip - bringing the *Vast* all the way back to Provincetown. It's a thrill to drive this 78-foot ship throttled up, out around the Peaked Hill Bars, and more slowly through the fleet of whales and whale watch boats. I don't mind slowing down to keep the whales safe; it's a magic time. Whales are spouting all around, and a few breach the surface nearby, their great blue-gray backs and classic humps showing clearly in the waning day. Several of the crew come out on deck to snap photos. I'm enjoying every minute of it.

The 2011 season had both thrills and disappointments. As Barry Clifford relates, "We spent 10 grueling days trying to expose a huge metallic anomaly, not necessarily magnetic (and not necessarily iron) from beneath the spot where we excavated the so-called "cannon pile" of 13 cannon excavated in 2009."

Unfortunately, they could only expose the very tip of this huge anomaly since their equipment just couldn't get them any deeper into the sand. "Things got even more frustrating after shifting our position to a new area approximately 50 feet downstream from "the cannon pile" and found concreted stacks of coins and 3 silver map rollers and gold dust all over the place. To me, this meant that the coins were still stacked together in chests when they went into the sand, thus leading us to believe that we may be approaching a level where intact or semi-intact chests might be found," Barry continues. The captured pirates testified at the time they were tried that the money was kept in bags in chests between decks. So it is quite possible that the treasure is under the guns in the "cannon pile."

This anomaly, which could be multiple chests of silver coins (as there is still nearly four tons of it down there somewhere), is approximately 10 feet below the "cannon pile." "We had gone back to this location with the intention of cleaning-up any gold dust or coins that may have been under the cannon, but instead discovered a completely new layer of wreckage much deeper than we could have imagined," Clifford says.

"After ten long and frustrating days of digging on this spot, akin to digging a building foundation with an ice cream scoop...we could only expose the very tip of the target. And while divers could actually see and touch the concretion, which they described as exceptionally hot to their hand held metal detectors, and certainly not a cannon, our equipment just couldn't dig any deeper."

The team also discovered a huge pre-glacial clay bank formation adjacent to the cannon pile, where divers observed caves and crevices that might act as catch-basins for coins and small objects. They recovered two more cannon, and know of at least four more in the vicinity of this bank.

Now, back at the dock, I step off onto the pier with my seabag, and Barry leans out the window of the bridge. He asks me what I thought of the trip. I reply that it was a great adventure, especially since the divers brought back some remarkable artifacts – real pirate treasure. Barry grins and calls out, emphatically, "People don't understand how much work it is to get this stuff!" He's right. But for him and for the crew of Expedition *Whydah*, it's worth all the sweat and effort, every minute of it!

◆◆◆◆◆◆◆

Autumn Romp in an Egg Harbor 41

"Memory Lane" isn't just the driveway leading to a nursing home, nor is it necessary the private road of the elderly. In fact, it can be a fun route to travel if you're cruising with an old boating buddy and swapping reminiscences of water-borne hijinks and intemperate times as you zoom past the islands, harbors, shoals and beaches where they took place. Memory Lane, one Friday afternoon in October of this past year, just happened to be a frothy wake running down Vineyard Sound in Massachusetts, where my friend Bruce and I were bringing a gently-used Egg Harbor 41' from Yarmouth, Cape Cod to its home for the winter in Fall River, Mass., a journey of perhaps seventy miles.

Seventy miles is a long journey at 11 knots, 13 with the current (occasionally), so there was plenty of time to come to a greater understanding of where misspent youth and, unfortunately, misspent adulthood come together, the pump usually primed by the experience of boating. Not that the Egg Harbor did not have the inherent capability of greater speed, but the leisurely cruising pace was entirely the fault of the port engine, which threatened a China Syndrome-like meltdown when or if I tried to push her over 1600 rpm.

Engines are, of course, humorless things. When they tell you something, they mean it; it's a no-nonsense conversation. Bruce and I were on the flying bridge, the only place to steer or navigate the big heavy tub, while cold wind blew in around the failed zippers of the isinglass enclosure. Bruce was steering (once on the helm, it is quite nearly impossible to pry him off), but I pushed by him and grabbed the Morse controls and throttled her way back. We had just left Hyannis harbor, after refueling, filling both swimming-pool-sized diesel tanks to the tune of $1,400 and were anticipating a brisk passage down Nantucket Sound. The cold Northwest wind was howling under a clear blue sky and whitecaps topped every wave.

"What? What's the matter?" Bruce asked, surprised at my sudden, urgent action.

"Look behind us," I explained, as a cloud of steam billowed astern as though someone had burst a boiler. The engine temperature gauge was up to 240°F. "Port engine's overheating. Got to throttle back and see if we can cool her down."

"Oh (expletive)," Bruce replied. "There goes our 25-knot romp down the Sound."

"And that's the engine that Billy said he just put the new raw-water impeller into the other day."

My friend Billy is a boat broker who specializes in 'flipping' boats. He'll buy an older boat dirt-cheap from some poor old fellow who can't take care of it any more, or from his widow, who is delighted that she now will never again have to set foot on the damned thing, and does a little bit of fix-up and then sells them for a profit. Usually they are older boats somewhat neglected; they've been sitting at the dock for some time, out of fuel, needing an oil change and a lot of various repairs to this and that. But they need to be brought to his marina so that they can get hauled, get a power wash and a coat of paint slapped on, and the RACORs changed. That's why Billy calls me; he needs a Captain who can somehow bring in and land these shot-up B-17s on his airfield without turning them into fireballs when they touch the tarmac. Most of the time, the engines run. Sometimes there are sails that can be set. There are usually no electronics that work or work right, cabin lights don't work or work intermittently, the head has something dead in it, and the icebox or reefer, if the boat has one, is full of gray mold as thick as moss and the remains of something that might have been a sandwich once upon a time. But that's the life of a delivery captain and I have to admit that I love it despite its occasional lump-in-the-throat trips.

We picked Bruce up at the Woods Hole ferry dock; he came over from the Vineyard just to cruise with me on this trip. Bruce and I don't get the opportunity to sail together very much these days for many different reasons. But only a few years ago we used to sail these waters from Cape Cod to Montauk and every place in between rather frequently on my boats, his boats, and anyone else's boat that we could finagle a berth on. He always showed up in the proper attire, and with the proper gear; rumpled old yellow oilskin jacket, shorts, boat shoes with no socks, sunglasses and croakies, ball cap, ditty bag, and a beat-up hand-held cooler full of cans of warm beer. No need to bring anything else, because whatever else was needed would be found on board, or somewhere else along the way.

At the marina, Billy climbed down into the engine compartment, with its very low overhead, and I followed. The big 450-horse Caterpillar diesels sat idle as we confirmed the location of switches, valves, filters, and shutoffs. Everything looked fine. He cranked over the diesels, and as they roared to life, a thick cloud of smoke arose and enveloped the boat. In spite of the day being windy, the suffocating fog of choking, acrid blue exhaust seemed to cling to the boat. I'd never seen such a pair of stinky, smoky, rumbly diesel engines. I wanted to get off that dock in a hurry, but I had work to do first.

A thorough examination of the bridge turned up not a single 12V outlet plug to allow me to run my notebook computer and charting program. Nope; we'd have to use the big, outdated chart-plotter that the boat already had. Unfortunately there were no charts loaded into it, and the card slot was empty. So all we got was a big fractal image with no appreciable detail and no real accuracy. We found out later that the radar didn't work, but we did have a depth sounder and a VHF radio. That was good news. There was also a big hand-held halogen spotlight, but it was useless because its 12V plug needed an outlet, and there was not a single one to be found.

On top of that, I had brought only a few food items that I grabbed before I ran out the door. Two apples; a blueberry tart from the nice Portuguese bakery in Warren; two pieces of fried fish fillets from the night before, breaded and chilled; and a dozen Italian pepper bread sticks, crunchy, crispy, and spicy. Nothing else. A thorough search of the galley did turn up several unopened bottles of water, cans of soda, and a candy bar. We would survive.

The engines still smoked like chimneys even after they had warmed up, so I was happy to finally ease her out into the very narrow, shallow Parker's River, just east of Hyannis. It was high tide, thank goodness; I hadn't developed a feel for the boat yet, so despite my most ginger application of her rudders and twin screws, she waltzed down the river with a noticeable skew, a bit of a zig-zag, and I hoped no one was watching as I carefully avoided the docks and private structures to my left, and the eelgrass and shallows immediately to my right. Another big cruiser was motoring up the river; I managed to get my boat's motion straightened out just before we passed each other, since I did not wish to appear 'green' at the helm!

I managed, without mishap, to bring her to the fuel dock in Hyannis, and was happy to fuel up as quickly as I could and be under way again, since the late-season day was waning. I did not want to be out on the water after dark. But once we had to slow down to 'baby' the port engine, I knew that we were going to make a portion of our passage in the dark. This would be difficult without a spotlight, the radar, or my detailed chartplotter. We would be feeling our way blind, with only our experience, our local knowledge, and our depth sounder. Happily, the big tub drew no more than four feet.

After running down Nantucket Sound from Hyannis, in clear, crisp weather, we cruised on past West Chop, East Chop, and entered Vineyard Sound. The tide was with us; we reached 13 knots as we straddled the middle of the current. The wind was moderating nicely; the whitecaps were gone. Bruce recalled the time when he had caught a bluefish right here, near the Middle Ground, while trailing a lure off the stern of my old gaff-yawl *Privateer*. We passed Tarpaulin Cove, where we have anchored in a norther before; through Quick's Hole and past Cuttyhunk Island, where we have boiled many a lobster in a big pot on the galley stove in his boats and mine.

While Bruce took the wheel, I went below to take a few moments to look through the boat, check the engine compartment, and make sure that things were generally in order, and they were. She was aging, built during the mid-1980s, a bit outdated, and needed work. But she was spacious, stable, and comfortable, with a fine layout forward, two cabins with comfortable upholstery and a wood-warmth that made me wish I could simply drop anchor for the night and have a comfortable sleep aboard in the port side double-bunked cabin. Water-stained wood trim beneath the large tinted cabin windows of the main saloon and no working cabin lights – except one – reminded me that she was in need of much attention and care. I hope she finds a new owner who will do a good job and spend enough resources to fix her up right, I thought to myself. I've a soft spot in my heart for grand old boats that have been sadly neglected.

The sun was setting behind clouds at the entrance to the Sakonnet River, and we still had the better part of sixteen miles to go to reach our destination at Fall River. There will be no moon tonight, I remembered, and with encroaching overcast from the west, it would be a dark night to boot. A couple of miles into the river, and I had to throttle her back again, and slow her down. I couldn't see the small nun and can buoys in the darkness, and collision with one could easily punch a hole in the hull. The Sakonnet is a winding river with many small but solid channel marker buoys, some shallows, but generally deep enough to handle this power boat. My only concerns were getting too far out of the channel and running aground, hitting a buoy, and navigating the congested Tiverton Basin with all the new bridge work going on, work barges and obstructions, and the very narrow channel through the cut where the old Stone Bridge was washed out in the hurricane of 1938.

We made it through, though, and happily into Mount Hope Bay, but the good Lord only knows how we never grazed a buoy, because there are quite nearly a dozen of them along the route. We did pass one large bell close aboard to port, and another that we heard ringing, but never saw in the murk. At last we reached the deserted marina, and by now there was no wind, only a tidal current to reckon with, and using that to our advantage, softly kissed her against a long floating dock on the inside of the slip area and made her snug for the night.

It was by now 7:30 in the evening, and my truck was parked there at the marina. I still had to drive Bruce back to Wood's Hole to catch the last ferry to the Vineyard, and then find my own way home, in by ten, to wife and hearth, a light snack, and a cold Guinness. My head found the pillow the same way that our boat sidled up against the floating dock; easily, gently, but without hesitation, and without any doubt about the direction that it was going!

◆◆◆◆◆◆◆

Ampy Saves a Pram

I grew up in and around boats. My grandfather Andrew, whose nickname was always 'Amp', had been a boat-builder and had worked for the Herreshoff yard in Bristol, Rhode Island; he began working there just before the Second World War. During the war years, when the famous yacht yard was given over to the war effort, he helped build Patrol Torpedo, or PT, boats.

For a number of years he had built small boats in his basement, much to my grandmother's chagrin. Boatbuilding was, and still is, a very time-consuming affair, and occasionally noisy and saw-dusty. At least he knew enough to build small enough boats so that they could be removed from the basement without having to take the house apart. But over the years he always owned a boat of some kind, usually power boats, kept them out in the backyard and worked on them there, scraping, painting, waxing, and alternately hammering on the engines. He was a true fixer-upper, a handy guy who could repair anything in or around a boat or around the house. In the summer, we always had the means to get out onto Narragansett Bay, to go cruising, or fishing, or just knocking about, for in the end it really was all about just being out on the water. We were not wealthy people, and did not own yachts, but because Grampy was a boat builder, we always had some type of craft to venture out on the bay in.

I barely remember Grandpa's Popeye-ish little motor boat, Fish Tales. This was an open-cockpit boat some twenty-odd feet long with a hull shape more like that of a sailboat than a power boat, a sea-kindly rounded hull tapering back to a smaller transom, with an engine box in the middle of the cockpit and a simple small gasoline engine installed under it. It was an "in-board" engine, and Grandpa steered the boat with a bronze tiller.

For shelter, *Fish Tales* had a bent wooden folding dodger-type rig that could be raised in a rainstorm, with a canvas cover, that created a cuddy half-cabin and would provide some minimal shelter from the weather. *Fish Tales* also had a wooden mast, although I don't ever recall seeing a sail hoisted. I was barely a toddler at the time and I was told, years later, that as a baby, I had often been put on top of the engine box, since it was a flat, convenient place to put a baby, and had slept there quite comfortably when the boat was under way; thus do we make motorboat men. I only recall one trip in *Fish Tales*, in the summer, to the beach at Hog Island, which is not more than two miles from the anchorage, but might have been all the way to Europe, for all that it seemed. Grandmother was aboard, as was my uncle Jed, my mother's brother, and on the way to the island, the sky became dark with an afternoon squall, and it began to rain fat warm droplets on the boat and everyone. I was but a small boy then, and I still recall the rain coming down hard, and Grandmother's voice, saying "Amp, I think it's starting to rain," and thinking that it was already raining quite heavily. But somehow that squall passed and we ended up on the shore of Hog Island, picking up driftwood, and Uncle Jed chopping whitened pieces off a large driftwood tree that had long been weathering above the high-tide mark. That is far back as my poor old addled mind can remember; it has been nearly a half-century since then, after all.

While I was still a young lad, Grandpa would bring me to the boatyard where he worked, occasionally, on a Saturday or a Sunday, when he was working on his own boat. He had acquired a big wooden cabin cruiser that had been built in the 1920s; these were the early '60s, now, and he was fixing it up. He'd cut a deal and acquired the old cruiser it for a very reasonable sum. It was the biggest boat that he had ever owned, perhaps forty feet long or more, and he was determined to fix it up and get it into the water to take his family out on. But when he first bought it, it had been neglected for a long time, and was up on blocks and boat stands in Mr. Pearson's boatyard, its seams yawning and the hull much in need of caulking, painting, and just plain wetness. For weeks one spring, after work, the caulking hammer pounded and the irons rang out like channel buoy bells in the early dusk, as long strands of soft tawny cotton were twisted and gradually fed into the seams, then hammered out of sight. The last whack of the hammer was always the one that rang true; it had a certain tone, I noticed, and when it achieved that tone, Grandpa moved the iron ahead in the seam another iron-length.

I asked Grandpa what he was going to name the boat; "*Fish Tales*," he answered; it was the same name that his other boats had carried over the years. One afternoon he was busy with a putty knife, forcing some thick reddish goop into the seams where he had pounded the caulking. I asked him what the stuff was; "Compound," was his one-word answer. He was not going to try to explain to a little boy what compound was all about, or why it was used; there was no point. I was to learn all of this much later.

Boatyards were interesting places. In the springtime, they were always worlds of strange odors. Back then, copper bottom paint had something of a pleasing, oily aroma, not like the synthetic antifouling polymeric stuff they formulate today that stinks horribly and makes one queasy with its smell. There was also the odd stench of curing fiberglass resin, polyester resin. To me these were the two scents that said 'boatyard' to me. The boatyard was a dangerous place though, with splintered wood, fiberglass, gooey stuff on the ground and upward-pointing rusty nails to step in and on. Grandpa often brought my cousin Mack and I to the boatyard while he worked. Mack was Uncle Jed's son and a year or so younger than I was. Grandpa did not like us to go wandering off; but we often did, as there was not much excitement in watching Grandpa work, at least not after the first ten minutes had passed.

We were told not to bother other men working on their boats, to stay away from them lest we should become troublesome or distracting. The weeds grew amazingly tall in the boatyard; long, discarded scraps of wood became swords. Once, we 'borrowed' a wooden ladder that was resting up against a boat. We did not realize that there was a fellow working inside the boat, but Grandpa soon knew it, and knew who was responsible, when he heard the fellow hollering across the boatyard for his ladder so that he could climb down. The other great thing about the boatyard was that it was a man's, and a boy's, place. If you had to pee, well, you went behind a boat where no one could see you. Grandpa had told us that this was okay. This was an act almost sacrilegious to us lads; there was something very naughty and at the same time appealing in this freedom to make water on tall weeds in the outdoors without catching a scolding or spanking for it; so whenever we could, we peed in the boatyard. It was a symbolic act of male liberation.

During those years, Gramp had a close friend named Russ. They had been friends since boyhood and were both members of the local Yacht Club. Now mind you, this was a blue-collar Yankee 'Yacht Club' where the members, in general, had absolutely no respect for fops or 'yachties' as the archetype is known even today. The old Yankee gentry who pretty much ran the place were taciturn old fellows who dressed in faded jeans and cracked oilskins, drank a little scotch, and had plenty of money, mostly old money, but you wouldn't know that any one of them wasn't a farmer at first encounter. There were also a few nouveau riche who pretended to be movers and shakers; they were always a bit more outspoken than the older class, but they had no real money, just a lot of debt and attitude, and a fondness for faded Nantucket red trousers and blue blazers. These were folks who had moved into town fairly recently and drank mostly gin, and lots of it, at the little yacht club bar, so much so that by the middle of a Saturday afternoon, the color of their cheeks matched that of their pinkish-red pants.

Then there were the vast majority of club members, most of whom were ordinary Bristol guys like Russ and Grandpa, who mostly sat out on the deck or on the lawn in wicker chairs with their wives and drank beer. These were the regular members and they were mostly small boaters and locals. It was a point of pride that reciprocal privileges were not extended to our club members by hoity-toity clubs such as New York Yacht Club, which essentially did not recognize our club's existence. That was fine with the BYC folks; after all, our members thought, who would want those folks coming down from their Newport mansion annex and hanging around here?

Russ had an old-fashioned motorboat, smaller than big *Fish Tales*, and used to take us out in it, Gramp, Mack, and me. I remember, in particular, the wonderful coziness of the forepeak, with its old-wooden-boat smell of paint and oil, musty, but feeling solid with the old exposed bent oak frames and planks, under the foredeck, dark, hiding away, feeling the up and down motion of the bow as I nestled in there on a cool spring morning, hearing the slosh of the water around the bow and feeling the gentle vibration in the hull as the old Chrysler flathead gasoline engine busily labored away with a steady thrumming. Looking aft, I could see through the length of the cabin and out on deck, Russ standing next to the big shiny bronze tiller, steering; and I could hear Gramp and Russ talking loudly over the sound of the engine and laughing. Mack was out there with them in the bright sun, sipping an orange soda through a straw. That is something that always stays with you; the sound, the smell, the feel of a snug wooden motorboat, the kind that would do no more than six to eight knots comfortably, but that was plenty fast enough and in fact at times too fast.

Grandpa never launched big *Fish Tales*. He became very ill quite suddenly that spring and, though he recovered, the boat had to be sold to pay medical bills. We had many other boating days with Grandpa in later years as we grew up, but always in smaller and more manageable boats. Grandpa never took on a boat project of that size again.

One summer afternoon, Gramp took Mack and me out bluefishing in Bristol harbor in Gramp's eighteen-foot flat-bottomed motor-boat. It was a plywood "sharpie," hard-chine, a simple boat with an outboard motor and a tiller extension. Mack and I sat on the thwarts and trolled for bluefish with our 'boat poles', old-fashioned fiber-glass stubby poles with casting reels that you really couldn't cast with unless you had a lot of sinker on the end of the line and you weren't afraid of getting a friction burn on your thumb when you cast. Gramp always loaded those reels with yellow woven squid-ding line. When you did cast, if you didn't restrain the spool, your reel would overspin and create a hopelessly tangled 'bird's nest' from which there was no recourse but to cut away half of your line. So we mostly trolled while Grandpa steered, put-putting slowly along.

On that particular day, we weren't catching anything, the day was warm, and thus we ventured out further, around the backside of Hog Island, near the little black and white fireplug of a light-house that was the only visible part of Hog Island Shoal above water. It was a fine day, sunny and bright with blue skies above, and we decided to break for lunch, going ashore in the little sheltered cove of Hog Island's southeast end. The beach is a sandy crescent that faces the north and the arm of the point reaches around to the northeast and shelters the little harbor from the prevailing south-westerlies. The water in the cove is shallow but the bottom soft and sandy and it was easy for Gramp to bring his flat-bottomed skiff in right to the beach. We had a thermos jug of punch, or 'bug juice' that Grandma had mixed up, some potato chips and tuna salad sandwiches, just the right stuff for a little picnic, and a couple of ripe purple plums. Grandpa anchored the boat in the shallows, just far enough out so that we wouldn't be beached by the tide, and we jumped over the gunwale in our bathing suits and water shoes – Grandpa always referred to the bathing suits as 'trunks' and our bat-tered sneakers as 'tennis' - and splashed and slogged our way to the beach with our picnic lunch bucket.

There was a great gray weathered driftwood log on the beach that was large enough for us all to sit on, and it was right in the shade of the only tree on the island's southeast point, a great green inverted bowl-shaped dark leafy tree of some kind that I didn't know, but whose dense cap of foliage created a wonderful shady bell of coolness that sheltered us from the hot sun but allowed the salty breezes off the bay to bathe us. Something about the fresh breezes made the food taste wonderful. It carried with it not just the tang of salt air but the wild sweet fragrance of beach roses, or Rosa Rugosa, in bloom; it was a combination that one never forgets and I sometimes imagine that I can smell the aroma in my sleep, especially when I am ill, and somehow I know that if I can smell it, I will always wake up feeling better.

After lunch, Mack and I decided to take a little walk on the beach, to do a little beachcombing; Grandpa had taught us the value and fun of that; one never knew what one might find, from old lobster trap buoys to driftwood and fragmented lengths of multicolored rope and line to odd shells cast up from the deep. The prevailing southwesterly breeze was beginning to pick up; and it did that every summer day just before noon, as the land heated with the sun's energy and the updrafts began drawing in the cool breezes off the bay and in from the ocean beyond. That was fine, though; it would freshen, by mid-afternoon, sometimes blow rather briskly and set up a good chop, but it was a breeze that would be behind us going home, pushing us along, and would even help us once we pulled up the anchor, gently nudging Grandpa's skiff out into deeper water where we needed to be to run the engine, without the need for any strenuous efforts or rowing or poling on our part.

So Mack and I went off adventuring while Grandpa sat on the driftwood tree trunk and smoked his pipe. He always let one of us boys pack his corncob pipe with the sweet Cavendish blend that he liked. It was a privilege, even if we never got the chance to puff the pipe ourselves, and both Mack and I had become rather adept at loading the pipe with just the right amount of tobacco, pressed to the correct density to burn well and evenly.

We stumbled and ran along the rocks, and at some point, Mack cried out, "Look, there's a boat washed up." We hurried up to it; it was a sorry-looking beat up old plywood pram, the paint all peeling off of it and generally weathered away, sitting upright and very dry and nestled in the dried band of cast-up seaweed and salt hay that ran along the beach above the high tide mark. This band of debris always ran a couple of feet higher, where the storm-cast flotsam and jetsam of bad weather rest until they rot away, or the next big

157

storm pushes them beyond the beach, beyond the berm of whitening slipper-shells and mussel shells at the highest point of the beach and into the salt-marsh beyond. We looked the derelict boat over carefully; it was not tied to anything, and appeared to have been resting there for some time. Scrawled on the little transom, perhaps painted with an old brush and sloppily done, was the barely discernible name "Me Toy", and nothing more. There was one piece of hardware, a rusted iron ring bolt, fastened through the flat bow-panel of the pram. The little boat, barely eight feet long, might have been painted black, gray, or dark blue, or each one of them, at one time or another.

We ran back to Grandpa, who was still sitting on the log, smoking and looking off into the distance at the green and sloping distant shore of Bristol. "Gramp, there's a shipwreck on the beach!" I exclaimed, excitedly. I wanted to be the first to announce the find.

"But I discovered it!" Mack chimed up; "I saw it first!"

"So what," I said. "It was my idea to rescue it."

"I want it!" Mack whined, and I almost thought he was going to cry, for the telltale bottom lip began to protrude in a pout.

"Oh big baby," I said.

"Hey now, you guys stop that," Gramp scolded. "What did you find? A boat? Let's go have a look. Come on, get along with one another."

Grandpa hiked over the beach to the boat with us, for it was only a hundred yards or so away. When we arrived, he stood next to it for a moment without saying anything, first puffing his pipe thoughtfully, then poking and scratching at it with his folding knife. He had an old rigging knife that he carried in his trouser pocket all the time, and now he alternately scraped parts of the boat with the blade, pried at the seams, and then poked the lethal-looking little folding marlinspike on the other end of it into holes and soft spots.

"Hmm. Ripe as a plum," he muttered.

"What's that, Grandpa?"

"Oh, nothing. Naaaah." He spat a tobacco-brown stream of spittle onto the shell-litter of the beach. Then he asked us to stand on either side of the pram and lift. It was not very heavy, actually, but to a couple of small boys, it seemed so, so we carried it a short distance at a time, dragged it some, staggered along with it some more, until we finally brought it, what seemed an interminable time later, to the shore of the little cove on the opposite side of the point, where we had come ashore.

Gramp brought the anchor up and then tied a line from the stern of his boat onto the ringbolt on the battered pram. Mack and I could see that the pram was leaking quite a bit. Gramp got the engine going and we quickly began heading out of the cove and into the more open water of Bristol Harbor. For a while, the pram towed along behind the boat nicely, surfing along, but Mack and I, in our orange life vests, sitting on the thwarts and looking aft at the pram, could see that it was riding lower in the water all the time. Mack and I wondered if we would make it back to the boat ramp with the pram or if it would sink down and out of sight and maybe even pull us down with it. The afternoon breeze had freshened and had set up a good chop in the harbor. Even though we were riding with it, it was bumpy water, and to compound matters, the pram soon swamped, and was very difficult to control. It dived and broached, capsized and rolled, much like a live, reluctant, big fish on the end of a fishing-line, being towed in. Grandpa had to slow the boat down, and it took all his skill as a boatman to keep us moving without being 'pooped' from behind by the stiff, choppy seas, or having to cut the pram loose to keep his boat from swamping. After what seemed forever, we brought the pram in to the dinghy launching ramp at the yacht club, turned it over and dumped the water out of it, and then – for it was much heavier now for having been wetted for an hour and soaking in the sea – Gramp helped us put it up on the shell driveway upside-down where it would dry out for a couple of days before he came down again in his old Ford Country Squire station wagon where we would load the pram partly into it, partly onto the tailgate, and tie it down. Then, Gramp, Mach, and I brought it home to his house, where it was immediately put up on sawhorses out under the big maple tree in the far southeast corner of the backyard.

Grandma just shook her head disapprovingly, a sour look on her face, as she stood in the doorway of the screened-in porch facing the yard, watching us carry our beat-up old treasure out back. "Now Andrew," she addressed him. "Not another one! Not another old piece of junk!" she scolded, with special emphasis on the last three words. Mack and I cringed, but Gramp puffed his pipe and ignored her remark.

As we were standing around the little derelict, staring at it admiringly, Grandma called us in for a bowl of chowder that she had just made. Grandma always made the best Rhode Island-style

clam chowder, not creamy but grayish-clear in color, strongly fla-
vored and seasoned with lots of black pepper, celery, onions, and
her secret, a few pinches of poultry seasoning. Of course, there
were lots of chopped fresh quahog clams and their juice in it as
well. She would also serve saltine crackers with it, or nice bakery-
fresh Portuguese bread rolls and butter. We all sat down and ate; she
did not ask about the pram; she already knew everything there was
to know about it from past experience.

"The first thing you do," Grandpa began explaining the next
day, when we were gathered with him next to the pram (and had
dutifully packed his pipe with Cavendish), "is to rip away all the rot
and bad stuff, and see what you've got left to work with." We were
excited, and we listened attentively.

As the ensuing days passed, Grandpa ripped away the old
wood, the broken pieces of gunwale and such, and made new ones.
He scraped, sanded, and filled the plywood sides and bottom
halves, and under his careful patient work, surrounded by the aroma
of blue pipe-smoke, the pram gradually began to look new again,
took proper shape, and when it was finally painted a medium blue,
it was beautiful, with new bronze oarlocks and hardware. It sat on
the water like a little blue duck and Mack and I took turns rowing
it around the dock at the yacht club under Gramp's watchful eye.
What had been old and cast-off had been made like-new again, and
the whole idea of being able to do that fascinated me. The little
pram skimmed along and bobbed on the afternoon waves in the harbor, light, graceful, and strong. It was wonderful, I felt. Gramp had
taken something dead and brought it to life, and I wanted to learn
to do that, too.

◆◆◆◆◆◆◆

www.ingramcontent.com/pod-product-compliance
Lightning Source LLC
Chambersburg PA
CBHW020245150626
46552CB00020B/414